Call It Consequences

"A super fun story and an even better protagonist. Both make this book un-put-downable. If you read only one YA book this year, make it this one!"

BRAD PAUQUETTE

#1 BEST-SELLING AUTHOR OF **THE NOVEL MATRIX**

"Alli Prince has written a story with enough depth to make a grown man cry and enough snark to delight the sassiest teenager."

NOAH MATTHEWS

AUTHOR OF **OUTLAW BLOOD**

"A thrilling ride through time and page, *Call It Consequences* is a novel that pulls at the heartstrings and captures the pain of growing up and letting go."

THIRZAH

AUTHOR OF **ADVENTURES IN ELDNAIRE**

CALL IT
CONSEQUENCES

Alli Prince

THE PEARL

PEARLMAG.CO

DEVELOPMENTAL EDITOR

Brad Pauquette & Lucy Grecu

COPY EDITOR

Lucy Grecu

BOOK DESIGNER

Noah J. Matthews

COVER ARTIST

Levi Matthews

Paperback ISBN: 978-1-960230-24-9

Ebook ISBN: 978-1-960230-26-3

Dedication

This book is dedicated to my father, who, upon my saying,
"I need you to tell me about tachyons," responded with,
"Ah, tachyons. I love them so."
Couldn't have written this one without you, Dad!

One

THERE'S A BIRD IN THE KFC. I watch it flutter from window to window, thinking it's found a way out only for the glass to brush inches from its beak. Each time, it rears back, feathers ruffled. Its panicked chirping keeps me company as I wait at the counter, counting the seconds until I can clock out.

It's just a bird. Nothing important. I ask my manager, Barb, to get it outside. She mumbles something about needing a smoke break and *"if you care so much, you take care of it,"* and then waddles out the back.

I roll my eyes. It's such a hassle. *It's just a stupid bird. Nothing important.* I sneak to the back to find a cardboard box or something to trap it in. Just as I find an empty box by the drive-thru window, the bell by the door dings. *Just what I need right now...* I jump to my feet, step up to the counter, and drop the box to the sticky, brown-tiled floor.

"Hi, welcome in!" I call.

The bird breaks for the door. It nose-dives through the air, like Darth Vader's ship in the first movie. It slams into the glass. In a flurry of feathers, it drops to the ground, then lies in a motionless brown lump. One wing is bent at an odd angle. Its neck is twisted in a way that doesn't look natural. A lump forms in my throat, and I look away.

It's just a stupid freakin' bird.

I take the customer's order. By the time I'm done, I'm finally—*finally*—allowed to leave this dead-end, burnt-chicken joint and go home. Not that home is any better.

I clock out and sneak back into the kitchen. As I go, I snatch a large cup and walk briskly across the floor to the drive-thru window. Charlie is on the counter, hunched over and staring at his phone. Pimples dot his jawline, and bits of blond hair stick out from his upper lip like brittle pieces of hay—a *desperate* attempt at a mustache.

"Hey, Charlie," I greet him with a nod as I reach around him and set the cup under the pop machine. 7UP—no ice. I press the rim against the silver arm and watch as the white, bubbly liquid fizzes out of the dispenser and begins to fill the cup.

Charlie doesn't look up from his phone. His words come out like old acrylic paint that's globbed up in the tube as he scrolls. "...Heeey, Lorrie."

"It's Lorraine," I snap.

"So, let's say you're, uh…talking to this girl." Charlie straightens, eyes still glued to the glowing screen in his hands.

"Uh-huh." I continue to watch my cup.

"And she says, '*that's cool*' to everything you say." His eyes finally flick up from his phone screen to me.

I shake my head. "Hate to break it to you, but she's either busy or…*really* not interested in you."

"Oh." Charlie leans back against the pop machine with a frown. Then, under his breath, he mutters, "*harsh*."

The liquid bubbles up to the top. I pull it back, waiting for the fizz to die down. Still reaching around Charlie, I press the cup against the lever again to top it off, then pull it back and slap on the lid. I yank a straw from the holder on the counter and rip the tip off.

Charlie's looking at his phone again. "Are you sure?"

I press the straw to my lips and blow. The wrapper shoots off the end and smacks Charlie in the forehead. He looks up with a glare, and I grin.

"I'm sure. That's how us women communicate."

His nose scrunches. I push my straw into the cup, the plastic squeaking.

"See you later—oh," I add, "there's a dead bird stinking up

the front. Might want to take care of that—*before* Barb sees it and blames it on me."

Charlie grumbles as he jumps off the counter but grabs the broom and dustpan and shuffles to the front anyway. I shoot a quick glance around—Barb's probably still on her smoke break. I snatch a brown paper bag of chicken thighs before I head out the back. As the door slams shut behind me, I shut my eyes and take a deep breath—*freedom at last.*

But I only have a moment of peace before I spot the man in the black suit. I glower and take a sip of 7UP as I watch him push off his silver sedan and march across the parking lot toward me. The creep always wears a black suit, no matter how humid and muggy it is outside. I can already feel my black tank sticking to my back under my work uniform, and I grimace. *I really don't need this. Not today, of all days...*

"Evening, Miss Sullivan," he drawls, like he's that agent guy from *The Matrix*. He flicks a toothpick into the bushes and pauses a couple of feet away from me. I shift on my feet and face the parking lot.

"*Miller,*" I sneer. "Run out of paperwork to do?"

Out of the corner of my eye, I can see him clench his square jaw. He's about a head and a half taller than me, his eyes obscured by thick, black sunglasses. A small, white scar mars the top part of his left eyebrow. I've always wondered what happened to him. It was probably something stupid, like petting a stray cat or running into a bookcase as a kid.

"Funny." He doesn't smile. "I'm here to ask you some questions, Miss Sullivan."

"Oh, what a surprise," I mock. "What*ever* could you be asking me about this time?"

"Do you know what day it is?" Miller asks.

I feel my stomach clench. I bend down and set the bag of chicken on the ground. As I stand, I pull my phone out of my back pocket.

"Thursday." I bite my lip as I flick through my apps and pull up my texts. I click one of three threads and quickly type out a message.

Miller's buggin. What's ur ETA?

I hit send and click off the phone.

"Do you know why *this* Thursday is so unique?" Miller strolls until he's standing in front of me. I focus on the ironed tie that sits snugly around his neck—*seriously, who takes the time to iron a tie?* He tilts his head to the side. "I'm sure you do, Miss Sullivan... Will you make me say it?"

I'm not an idiot. I *know* why he's here. He asks the same

stupid questions every freakin' week, in that same stupid suit with that same stupid tie. It'd probably be better to just answer him—to talk about the awful, *pathetic* thing and be done with it. Instead, I force my lips into a tight grin.

"You decided to stop bothering me and wanted to wish me a final farewell?" I stare up at him. His expression doesn't change. I barrel on, "Oh, Miller, I will *so* miss our chats—"

"Eight years ago today, that's July 17th, 2010, your father, George Sullivan, and your mother, Jessica Sullivan, conducted an *unsanctioned* experiment with top secret Huson Laboratory equipment. This experiment violated their contracts with Huson Laboratory of Research and Development and resulted in the death of—"

"*I get it!*" I snap. "You don't have to remind me." I look away. I try to swallow past the sudden lump in my throat. My cheeks feel hot. I clench my fist. "What do you want?"

"Anniversaries are...*dangerous*. They bring up emotions that stir people to make idiotic choices." Miller lowers his sunglasses and leans down until we're staring eye to eye. "Your father wouldn't be making any *idiotic choices* today, would he?"

I clench my teeth. "Like I've already told you *hundreds* of times, my father gave up that project."

"No, he didn't." Miller straightens, his sunglasses back in place.

"Your father was forced to cease experimentation when he lost his top secret security clearance, was fired, and signed the NDA. I know I don't need to remind you of that either."

"And yet here you are," I mutter. My phone pings, and I glance down at the message.

Want me to punch him?

I roll my eyes and look back at Miller. I'm not sure what his job is, specifically. I only know that, after what happened, Huson Labs hired him to keep his ever-watchful eye on the Sullivan family. To ensure none of their *"precious research equipment"* winds up in the hands of regular people. Good ol' Miller has been a complete and utter pain in my neck ever since. He takes his job *way* too seriously and approaches every conversation like he's a special agent from the FBI. But I know what he really is: *a nuisance.*

"Lorraine," Miller drones, "your father is a recluse. He hardly leaves the house, except for every Tuesday and Thursday evening, when he walks around your neighborhood. It...makes Huson Labs curious about what he could be spending all his time doing—especially *today.*"

"Why don't you ask him?" I shoot back. "If you're so curious."

"We will, if we have to... Do you think we have to? Your father was not mentally well after the failed experiment. It wouldn't be hard for us to start another investigation, pull in the police, grab a warrant, raid the house...that is, *if* we suspect he's broken his agreements." Miller's voice is low, like he's speaking to a frightened child rather than the adult that I am. I let out a breath and straighten my shoulders.

"No, *sir*. Like you said, he's not allowed to run any further experiments..."

Mr. Miller frowns—a slight tug on the corner of his otherwise straight and stoic lips.

I cross my arms, take another sip of 7UP, then say, "That all you need?"

"One more thing." Miller takes a step back. He reaches inside his jacket and pulls out a tiny white card. He holds it in front of my face. "If you ever think your father is stepping down a path he shouldn't be on, *call me*. We'll just talk. I want to help you, Lorraine, if it comes to that."

I grunt and pluck the card from his outstretched hand. "Oh, *goody!* Another card to add to my collection. You'll have to start ordering these in bulk if you keep handing them out like this."

Behind him, I spot a blue pickup truck turning into the parking lot. Its sides are checkered with large spots of rust, and a single orange bungee cord holds the silver bumper in place.

I shove my phone and the card into my back pocket. "Catch you next Thursday, *Agent* Miller."

Miller, as usual, doesn't say goodbye or acknowledge the little nickname I've given him. Instead, he stands and watches the blue pickup screech to a stop in front of the KFC. I jog toward it. I wave my hand in front of my face and cough through the exhaust fumes, tug open the door, and slip into the cushioned fabric seat.

"You're late," I snap. My boyfriend, Buck, sits in the driver's seat.

"You didn't respond to my text," Buck whispers as he glares at Miller through the passenger door window. "Want me to punch him?"

I scoff, "Of course not—I just want to go home."

"Shoulda tased him."

"I left my taser at home. Can we just go? *Please?*"

"Okay," Buck mutters, then shifts the truck into drive. The whole thing rumbles as the engine splutters, and we speed away from the KFC and from Miller. Away from Miller's stupid tie and stupid, piercing questions.

Two

THE PICKUP RUMBLES DOWN the deserted backroads of Ohio. The windows are half down and music is stuttering from the radio. I curl up in the seat and close my eyes. I let the wind beat against my face as I lean my head against the side of the car. I tug off my hat, wincing as the Velcro rips out a strand of hair, and toss it on the floor. Next is my polo shirt. There's a split-second where I think, "*God, I hope I don't reek,*" but then I feel the wind against my sweat-soaked tank top, and I relax into the breeze. Still, I keep my arms down, just in case.

"You know," Buck yells over the wind, "you should really take your taser with you. Bought it for you so you could protect yourself from creeps like Miller."

I shake my head, a smile pulling at my lips. I didn't have the guts to tase someone—no matter how annoying they were. Besides, Miller might be annoying and inconsiderate—like a piece of gum stuck to the bottom of your shoe—but that doesn't make him dangerous. He'd probably sue me if I tased him. He seems like he's petty like that.

"So, how was work today?" Buck asks.

I shrug as I sit up. I lean forward and turn the radio down a notch, then settle back in my seat. "Barb was a monster about my name tag again. It's not like I'm even doing anything wrong—she just wants someone to punish." I huff and cross my arms tightly against my chest.

Buck raises a single eyebrow. I shift to look directly at him, raising a challenging eyebrow of my own. Buck's wearing an open red-and-black flannel shirt over a dark-gray tank top. His hair is mid-length and curly. He's only two years older than me, which seemed like a crazy big age gap when I was eighteen. Now, at twenty, I find I don't mind it as much. I glance at the freckle above the right side of Buck's lips. When we'd first met, I'd thought it'd been a smudge of chocolate. I'd told him to wipe it off. He'd laughed at me, thinking I was making a joke.

"I'm sure she just wants you to be your best, babe!" Buck yells, and I snap back to the conversation. Buck is always like that—all *positive* and *hopeful*. If all his happy-go-lucky-ness could power a generator, I'd never have to pay the electric bill again.

I roll my eyes, glancing out my window at the rocky terrain of the Appalachian Mountains. Well, we call them *mountains*, but they're really more like glorified hills. Every stone is strangled with life—roots and weeds and scraggly green bushes. It's all balanced out neatly with the roadkill. As we speed down the back roads, the sun casts a golden hue on everything it touches.

"How's your dad?" Buck asks, and I feel my heart tug against my ribs. I roll my eyes again.

"Who cares?" I mutter.

Buck raises another eyebrow and leans toward me. "What?" he shouts over the wind.

I press my lips together and roll up the window. Buck does the same, glancing at me expectantly.

"What?" I ask.

"Your dad—how was he before work today?"

"Don't know. Didn't ask." I shrug. "Hey, when's your job interview for Hyland Software again? That's this week, right?"

Buck glances at me from the corner of his eye and shakes his head. He knows I've already asked this.

"No, it's next week," he answers anwyay. "Did I tell you what Papa said last night?" he adds.

I sit up.

"He told me computers would make me soft—that I can't

trust tech 'cause it'll turn against me one day, and then I'll have nothing to show for my hard work. Can you believe that?" Buck chuckles under his breath. "I know it's just 'cause he doesn't want me going all the way to Cleveland..."

Buck frowns and starts to tap his fingers against the steering wheel. He shifts, nibbles on his bottom lip, takes a breath, then says, "But why didn't you ask your dad how he was before you left?"

"Because I *didn't*. Why are we talking about this?" I snap. "First, Miller interrogates me, and now *you*?"

Buck sighs. "I'm not interrogating you."

"Oh? Then what would you call this?"

Buck's grip tightens on the steering wheel. "Well, I would have called it a caring conversation, but it seems to have a bit of a bite to it now, don't you think?"

I frown and look at the floor of the truck. Straw and dirt cling to the grooves of the gray flooring. There's an old french fry nestled in the cup holder in the side of the door.

"I just...you lost your mom, but your dad lost a wife..." Buck mutters. "I'm sure both of you are grieving today. Forgive me for thinking it might benefit you to do that together."

A scowl worms its way onto my face and I refuse to look up at Buck, even though I can feel him staring at me.

"You *know* what he *did*, Buck."

"Lorraine—"

I whirl toward him. "He *killed* her."

Buck runs his hand through his hair. I watch as his fingers snag on the tangles. He tugs his hand the rest of the way through and switches to rubbing his forehead, staring at the road ahead of us. I can feel my cheeks heating—they're probably red like an electric stovetop someone's forgotten to turn off. Sweat slides down my back. I click my tongue and huff.

Finally, Buck raises a palm in surrender. "Alright, alright, I'm sorry…I just…I know what today is and I want to be there for you, you know? I'm sorry. You can tell me anything, I promise."

I frown. "Yeah."

"Seriously, babe—I'm here for you. Always," Buck says again, and this time I meet his eyes. The anger that's been simmering cools and my shoulders drop. There's a lightness in his eyes—an ease I can't even begin to describe.

"I know," I whisper.

Buck nods and for a moment the only sound is the radio. But then Buck grins.

"Hey," he nudges me with his elbow. "You know what would be fun? Donuts!"

I side-eye him. "What? We passed Dunkin's ten minutes ago—"

Buck slams on the brakes and the truck grinds to a stop on

the empty back road. I slide forward and I grab the handle on the ceiling.

"Buck!" I shriek. Buck lets out a wicked cackle, then holds the gas and the brake at the same time. He turns the wheel hard to the left and we start to spin. I hold onto the seat, a giggle escaping my mouth.

"Buck—*Buck,* what if someone comes?!" I crane my head, trying to see if there's anyone behind us. Buck throws his head back and hollers as we pinwheel in the middle of the street. The tires squeal against the road and I smell the burning of rubber. Smoke rises around us. Then, Buck shifts gears. He releases the brake. We shoot off down the road.

"That was illegal, you know." I snicker and smooth back my hair. Buck leans forward, scanning the road.

"Huh, weird," he says with a sly grin. "I don't see any signs against it."

I snort, then settle back in my seat. I can feel the smile that had taken over my face slip as we continue down the road. I can't ever forget what happened eight years ago, but sometimes when I'm with Buck, for just a moment or two, he helps it feel...I don't know. Better, I guess.

"You really should get us some donuts, though," I say. "That sounds good."

Buck chuckles. "Tomorrow, maybe." He glances at me and wiggles his eyebrows. "Unless you want to get into the driver's seat and actually practice your driving like we've talked about—get your hours for your license."

I wave him off. "Let's just go tomorrow."

Three

AS WE PULL UP TO MY HOUSE, I see my dad sitting on the porch steps. The street lamps have just clicked on, and the sky above is an array of soft pink clouds and faded blue skies. My dad sits with his phone to his ear—*what schmuck called and got stuck listening to Dad this time?* His eyes hide behind his Edna Mode spectacles, and his bushy brown eyebrows pull together as he speaks into his old flip phone.

I scrunch down in my seat as the truck rumbles to a stop. Our place is a small two-story house with a front porch—and at first glance it's a house you could almost be proud of. The front porch is made up of deep, rich red brick, and the roof is a decadent brown with matching chocolate trim. But the side paneling is in *desperate* need of a repaint. It clings to the outside of the house like barnacles on the underside of a ship. The bushes around the front are overgrown and thorny. I'm thankful we're nestled at the edge of town on a one-way street, with thick green trees to separate us from our neighbors.

On the opposite side of the street from us is an old field that has long since been abandoned. I used to sneak over there as a kid, but now the weeds are thick, crowding any sense of wonder or imagination that place used to hold. I'm pretty sure it's a wildlife haven for the deer—and with the deer come the ticks. *Hard pass.*

"Can I help you carry your stuff?" Buck asks as he shifts the truck into park.

"Nope." I reach down and scoop my belongings into my arms—the sweaty polo, the purse, the hat, and, finally, the brown bag of mediocre chicken thighs. I slip out of the truck and kick it shut.

I wince as my dad's voice rises from behind me. "That's what I've been saying! No, Sebastian—*listen to me!*"

I hope the trees block his voice. I'd hate to get a complaint from the neighbors. I turn on my heel and head toward the house.

My dad's pacing now, his arms motioning wildly in front of him even though whoever he's on the phone with *obviously* can't see him. He pauses as he reaches the porch swing and stops, meeting my eyes. A grin breaks out on his face. I try my best to smile back. I hear Buck shut the door to the truck and jump up the steps to catch up with me. He puts his hand on my shoulder and squeezes.

The volume on my dad's phone must be all the way up, because I can hear Sebastian Hartford's voice shouting from the other end.

"Do you care *nothing* for Einstein's Theory of—"

"Seb—*Sebastian*, I've got to go, Lorrie's home!" My dad pulls the phone away from his ear, and I hear Sebastian ranting from the other side until my dad snaps the flip phone shut.

Sebastian's an old coworker of my dad's—the only one to stay in touch with him after he was fired. As a kid I lovingly referred to him as "Uncle Seb." He came over almost every day after the accident to console my dad and ever so *helpfully* remind me I "still had a future." As if that is what every twelve-year-old wants to hear after their mom dies... Still, he *did* offer to pay my way through art school if I ever decided I was good enough to actually pursue that dream.

I didn't.

Seems pointless to waste his money on something like that now.

"Hey, Dad." I start up the steps of the porch. My dad rushes forward, arms open. I look up and raise my eyebrows. He stops for a moment, arms still up for a hug, then hurriedly drops them to his sides.

"I—you're home just in—I mean, how's work?" He slips his hands into his pockets.

I cringe and look away. "It was fine." I hold out the bag of chicken. "Here—I brought you dinner."

"Oh, thank you—and good, good, that's good to hear— Oh! *Buck*!" My dad throws his arms out again. Buck mirrors the expression, grinning.

"Dr. Sullivan!" Buck steps forward and the two men bear-hug, a gesture chock-full of quickly diminishing testosterone. I roll my eyes and hurry past them into the house.

The cool relief of the air conditioner washes over my arms, and I shut my eyes. I lean against the purple-painted wall and kick off both my shoes. Then I push myself up and walk to the middle of the hallway. I drop my purse by my boots and step to the left, into the family room.

My eyes fall on the mantel over the fireplace, on the far end of the room. But the mantel isn't what catches my attention—it's the urn on top of it, sitting next to a picture of my mom. I clench my fist and force myself to take a deep breath. I shove my emotions back into the tightly sealed mason jar they belong in and try to focus on something else.

A TV sits neglected in the corner of the room, blasting a FOX News reporter's monotone voice through the speakers. Looks like Dad left it on again—*does he care nothing for our electric bill?*

The reporter's holding a microphone under her chin. "Dozens

of protestors swarmed the streets last night, objecting to the latest technological research being conducted at Huson LABS," she drones. You can see the streets of Columbus behind her. "Protestors are claiming that the private research facility is conducting unethical experiments that harm the lives of humans and animals alike. CEO of Huson Laboratories, Victoria Huson, made a statement last night denying these claims, stating—"

I storm into the room, snatch up the remote, and stab the off button with my thumb. The screen stutters, then turns black. I toss the remote on the couch and stalk into the kitchen. Behind me, I hear the front door open.

"It's really—wow, I mean—do you have the time to see it? Because I'd just love to show you and Lorrie!" my dad rambles.

Buck, ever so patient, is listening with a grin. "Of course, Dr. Sullivan! We'd love to see it."

"No!" I call as I open the fridge, peering inside. "*We* don't want to see anything! If Buck wants to, that's fine, but I'm busy."

I'll need to go grocery shopping tomorrow if I want anything to eat over the weekend. I pull out the milk and give it a sniff, immediately grimacing as the sour smell hits my nostrils. I toss it into the trash on my left. On the floor next to the bin is a small cardboard box of junk—well, *my* junk. It's got some old art, a couple of college applications, and a purple flash drive.

I scoff. I'd asked Dad to take that out weeks ago. Trash day isn't until Tuesday, so there on the floor it will continue to sit. Typical.

Buck emerges from the hallway and hops onto the counter. He pulls two apples from the fruit bowl, rubs one on his shoulder, then sinks his teeth into the bright red skin. Juice slips down his chin as he tosses me the other. I catch it with one hand and glance it over. He always seems to know what I need—sometimes even before I do.

"Lorrie!"

"It's Lorraine," I snap, and my dad snaps his mouth shut. I walk over to the sink and run the apple under the cool water. I can practically feel my dad hovering behind me—waiting for me to invite him in, like he's a jobless, middle-aged vampire with astigmatism. Like this is *my* house, not his.

I close my eyes and take in another breath, then glance at him over my shoulder. "Dad—you named me Lorraine, so just call me that. I'm not a little kid anymore."

"I know, I know, I'm sorry. It's just...sorry." He mutters and looks at the ground. I follow his gaze. His shoelaces are untied. He shakes his head then motions to the stove. "I made you spaghetti. Just the way you like it."

I glance over at Buck, who is now pointedly looking up at the ceiling, gnawing thoughtfully on his apple. My stomach churns, and guilt curls its slender fingers around my ribs. I shut off the water and rub the apple dry on my jeans. I bite into it as I turn around and lean against the counter.

"Sho," I speak through the mouthful of fruit. Juice dribbles down my chin, and I wipe it off with my sleeve. "Wush 'ish thing you wanted to show me?"

My dad's eyes light up.

"I did it this time." Dad sighs deeply, like he's never been so sure of anything in his life. He rubs his hand over his beard and nods. "It's actually ready, I'm sure of it."

I cross my arms. "Yeah? *Prove it.*"

He grins. Then he's a flurry of limbs as he books it toward the living room. He fishes a golden key out of his pocket and snatches a throw pillow off the couch.

He shakes his head and sets the pillow back down. "I-I need something—something small to test it on."

I glance around the kitchen when an idea strikes. *My cardboard box of junk.*

"Here—" I scoop down and pick up the box. "Use this. Needs to be thrown out anyway." My dad rushes back in and grabs it from me, then stops and raises an eyebrow. "Your art? But... You loved these pictures—and your purple flash drive, isn't there—" Something changes in his eyes—there's a different sort of sheen

I haven't seen before. He picks the flash drive off the pile, holds it up, then looks back at me with a grin. "*Oh*—this is *perfect*! We can see if the integrity of the files remains the same—Lorraine, you're a genius!"

I'm *really* not. It's just a box of junk—and the flash drive? It's got nothing but old video diaries—a therapy technique to try and help me move on from the past. While it didn't technically help, it did make me feel better, you know, for a time... But they aren't something I'm thrilled to go back and watch. I barely even remember what's on them at this point—just a lot of raw pain and grief, I imagine. I'd decided to throw the flash drive out months ago, but had procrastinated until I finally ended up setting it in the box by the trash about two weeks ago. Two whole weeks for my dad to throw everything out.

I think about the Machine downstairs—the experimental piece of crap that takes up residence in our basement. They never turn out right, these experiments. They always destroy whatever's inside... Using my old junk as a guinea pig is as good of a way as any to destroy it. Besides...he's used *much* worse guinea pigs before...

Four

DAD LEADS THE WAY TO THE BASEMENT, Buck right behind him. I drag my feet as I follow. I watch as Dad unlocks the door. He always keeps it locked but I'm not really sure why. Don't know, don't care. This isn't going to work. It never does.

I follow Buck with my hands half in my pockets. Buck seems eager, which isn't abnormal but it's still annoying. He's practically bouncing on the tips of his toes as he follows my dad through the door and down the concrete steps. Maybe Buck's eager because he's only seen the Machine once before.

Instead of our house being a *regular* house with a *regular* basement, our place is multi-leveled and large. Dad built the house himself and spent hundreds of hours designing, redesigning, and eventually completing this friggin' basement. I remember wandering the half-finished basement as a small child, back before a house was on top of it.

We step off the staircase and walk into a large concrete room. The ceilings are vaulted, easily twenty feet above us. Small sections of the room are blocked off by makeshift cubicles, each filled with thousands of papers tattooed with my dad's chicken scratch writing. I briefly wonder how many trees had to die in order to make space for my dad's crazed thoughts and theories. Large wires, tubes, and extension cords are strewn about the floor, like winding black snakes, all slithering and writhing toward the Machine in the center of the room.

To the right are computers stacked on top of a standing desk, which is trapped behind a large plastic shield. That smudgy bit of plastic is the only safety precaution in this musty dungeon.

I lean against the wall next to the fire extinguisher and blow a piece of hair out of my eyes. Dad jogs halfway into the room, spins on his heel, and throws out his arms.

"Welcome to the Tachyon Implementation of Mass and Energy Machine!" my dad grins.

T-i-m-e Machine... I roll my eyes. It's a *TIME* Machine. Or it would be, if it actually worked.

Buck leans down to me. "Isn't your dad like...banned from working on this thing?" he whispers as Dad bounces toward the Machine, which trespasses upon half the room.

"Technically? Yes." I tap the fire extinguisher with my nails, then push myself off the wall. The night of the accident, Huson Laboratory came and took everything—his notes, his research, even his personal laptop. Since then, he's been obsessed with re-building the entire thing from memory. Testing, retesting, and then retesting again—over and over *and over*. It's all he talks about—all he thinks about. Maybe even all he cares about.

Finally, I force myself to look directly at the Machine.

At the center of the Machine is a circular metal platform. Sur-rounding it are giant metallic limbs. The inside of each arm puls-es with blue, then purple, then white light. They're secured at the bottom of the circular base, curving up and out like a ballerina's arm. They connect again above the metal platform. The shape of it all is strange, like nothing you'd find in nature. My dad could talk about the science of it—and he *is*, rambling *on and on* with Buck about what each part does and why—but to me it looks more like a bird's cage than anything else.

Hanging from the ceiling in a circle around the Machine, draping like jungle vines, are thick black tubes. All around the floor is a mess of wires and tubes, circling the Machine in the opposite direction from the ones hanging from the ceiling. The entire thing is indistinguishable from one giant tripping hazard. "So how is this different from the billion other times you've shown this to me?" I ask as I glance down at my nails. I need to repaint them—or at least stop chewing on them. They look awful.

"It's all about the tachyons!" My dad rubs his hands together like a fly.

"Tachyons?" Buck asks.

My dad nods and points to the thick black tubes. "You see, *years ago* we devised a way to harness them—well, more like observe them and try to convince them to go where we want. But now—I think now I've finally gotten them to go in the right direction!"

"How?" Buck's eyebrows shoot into his hairline. He's like a little kid on Christmas morning, only he's enraptured with the theories and ideas of time travel instead of candy canes and gingerbread.

I roll my eyes and turn away as Dad launches into an overly complicated mess of an explanation. I listen, barely able to catch each word let alone understand what they all *actually* mean strung together.

I'm not smart like either of my parents. While they'd been geniuses (literally, geniuses. Each had an insane IQ. My mom's was 153 and my dad's is 148), that trait had, unfortunately, breezed completely past me. I grew up hearing stories about my dad's childhood, how he'd taken apart the refrigerator and put it back together at seven. Me at age seven? I'd just doodled on the walls.

"Right," I say as Dad stops his impromptu science lecture. "Well go on, then. Show us what you so *desperately* wanted us to see."

"Put your box in the center." Dad nods to the Machine. I roll my eyes and gingerly step over the wires and tubes, careful not to trip. I duck under the big metal arms and put the box of junk on the circular metal platform. I pause for just a moment, staring at the center.

Mom had been standing there in her final moments—or so I'd been told. I don't remember much from back then. Being in the same room where my mom had taken her last breath should bother me. Maybe a part of it does, I don't know.

My dad rushes around the room, flipping switches and turning knobs. I walk back over to Buck, who's vibrating as he watches, a grin splitting his cheeks. Then Dad grabs my and Buck's arms and drags us behind the large plastic shield by the computer.

"Safety first!" Dad plops a helmet on my head, then moves me behind him as he fiddles with the control panel. If only he'd thought of safety eight years ago.

"Dr. Sullivan—are you sure this thing will keep us safe?" Buck pokes the plastic shield. It wobbles.

Dad reaches out and steadies it. "Perfectly safe." He's still focused on the small monitor to his right. "Just stay behind it. Now, before we begin, what's the first rule of time travel?"

I roll my eyes. "Time is fixed, don't play God," I drone. "Bad things happen when you play God."

"Exactly!" Dad says. "The ethics of time travel is like hiking through nature. Stay on the trail, leave what you find, and—under every circumstance—respect the wildlife!"

"The *what*?" Buck asks.

"It's a fancy way of saying don't talk to anyone you see," I huff.

Every time my dad launches an experiment, he launches into the same set of rules. Not like he's ever actually had the opportunity to break any of those rules.

"Now—we're ready!" Dad slams his fist down on a button. Immediately, the lights overhead flick off. In the dark I can see the glowing blue liquid in the tubes along the ceiling and floor. I watch as gears begin to turn, and a hum of electricity permeates the room. I hear the pipes in the wall gurgle. The tubes wiggle as the liquid flows in circles toward the Machine. A square light on the metal platform clicks on as the arms around the Machine's base begin to spin. I feel a pull at my core—something deep and instinctual—and I step toward the plastic shield.

I glance up at Buck. His eyes are wide, mouth parted. I shake my head and look back at the Machine. I can't help but think back to that night eight years ago. They'd told me I was there—that I'd witnessed it. Sometimes, it infuriates me that I can't remember. Other times, I don't know…maybe it's better this way.

I swallow and shut my eyes—I always do when he tests the Machine. I just can't bear to watch it. I can hear papers fluttering, the whir of the large metal arms as they spin faster and faster. I feel the hair on my arms begin to rise. A wave of heat washes over us. Buck slides his hand into mine.

"It's working!" my dad crows from beside me. "It's working! It's—"

I hear a discouraging zap of electricity and my eyes fly open. The Machine groans, the metal arms slowly stop spinning, and the lights overhead click back on. The Machine is dead. Again. *Shocker.* I step up to the shield, peering at the center. There's no box of old junk there anymore—just a pile of ash. Just like always.

"What happened? What went wrong?" Buck asks. My dad's hunched at the computer, his fingers clattering rapidly over the keyboard.

I let out a breath, my heart hammering inside my chest. I throw off the helmet and stalk toward the stairs. "Kay, this was… *fun* or whatever," I call over my shoulder, "but I'm done. Keep playing with your toys!"

"Lorrie—I mean, *Lorraine*! Lorraine, wait!" My dad stumbles after me. I take the stairs two at a time, my cheeks hot.

I *knew* it wouldn't work. It never does. *Ever.* My dad's spent the last eight years trying to fix his mistake, and for what? For nothing. He's never going to fix this—fix *us*.

My dad thunders after me into the living room. "Lorraine—"

"Do you know what day it is?" I ask, spinning around to face him.

He blinks dumbly, eyes wide. "Thursday, I think."

My mouth drops. "I don't believe you," I whisper. "For a 'time scientist' you're really bad at anniversaries."

Dad's face pales. "Is it your birthday?"

I throw my hands in the air and storm toward the stairs.

"Lorraine!" he calls. "Wait!"

"No!" I shout back. I lumber up the stairs and pause at the landing. My hands curl into fists. I turn to stare down at him. With teeth clenched and narrowed eyes, I sneer, "I knew it wasn't going to work. You wasted my time."

"No—Lorraine, if you would just have *faith*," my dad starts. I hold up my hand, and he snaps his mouth shut.

"Why believe in something if you *know* it will fail?" I challenge. I nod to the pictures on the wall—of the three of us before everything. "It always fails. This is why you were kicked off the board—why you were fired—why you shouldn't even be messing with that thing!"

My dad looks like I've just slapped him. I kind of wish I had. He stops on the bottom step, eyes wide. "Lorraine…" he whispers.

I shake my head and walk the rest of the way up the stairs. I slam my bedroom door behind me. It's stupid to be angry—especially because *I knew* it would fail. Maybe it was the anniversary. Maybe I'm still grieving…

Either way, Mr. Miller was right. People are stupid on anniversaries.

Five

I REST THE BACK OF MY HEAD against my bedroom door. My room is a converted attic space. The ceiling is raised on the left side and slants down until it meets the window seat on the right. That seat is chock-full of old stuffed animals I'd long since stopped playing with. In the middle of the room, the blankets rumpled and unmade, is my bed, the headrest pushed against the far wall. My dresser and mirror are to my left, though I hardly utilize them. Clothes are strewn about the floor, mostly clean or clean adjacent. Folding laundry is the worst—but only because I let it pile up until it's too big to handle.

I fish Miller's card out from my pocket and toss it on the dresser, next to the fifteen other identical cards he's *ever so graciously* gifted me through the years and the shiny black taser I'd gotten from Buck. I doubt I'll ever need to use either of those things.

I shrug off my work uniform, then grab the pair of pajama shorts I'd left on the floor by my bed and pull them on. Then I grab an old, faded t-shirt from the nightstand—the Avengers graphic is super cracked and faded, but the material is soft from wear. I shuffle through the mess to the window seat, where my laptop sits amidst the neglected stuffed animals. Jammed in the USB port is a smudgy black flash drive. I click open the video software. I used to use a camcorder to film, but the laptop is more convenient now—and, more importantly, password protected. I'd tossed the camcorder into a corner of my room... It's probably still there, dead and forgotten.

I stare at myself on the dusty computer screen. Faded freckles are splattered across my cheeks. Soulless brown eyes blink—I reach up my hands and wipe at the bags under them, as if they could vanish that easily. I haven't gotten a haircut in ages. It's grown well past my shoulders, tangled and ratty and oily black. *I need a shower.*

"Well..." I look into the little black eye of the camera in my laptop. "Today's been *such a blast.* Dunno why I thought this anniversary would be *any* different..." I hug myself and look away from the camera. My eyebrows pinch together and I clear my throat. "Dad's being his usual oblivious self. He tested his stupid machine *again.* I don't know why he bothers—and you won't believe what Mr. Miller said to me today! He just *had* to interrogate me, today of all days. I mean, *obviously*—he does this every week, so I shouldn't be surprised—but because it's the anniversary of *Mom's*—"

My voice cracks and I stop. I suck in a breath. Pause the recording. These usually helped, these videos. I don't know why I first started to film them, just...one day, after the accident, I grabbed the camcorder and poured myself into the hollow black eye. I never share the videos with anyone—I just save the files on a thumb drive. I must have collected hundreds of hours of me talking, crying, and sometimes even screaming at the camera. It used to be so therapeutic, but lately...I don't know, it just isn't enough.

It's why I threw out the first flash drive—the purple one that's now a pile of ash in the Machine. I don't want it around anymore—the evidence of my past, so to speak. I want to try and move—I *need* to try and move on.

I set my laptop next to my shark Squishmallow and roll off the window seat.

"Ugh, what a day," I groan. I press my palms against my forehead. I need to clean my room—clothes are everywhere, and there's a stack of dirty cups and a bowl of stale chips on my bedside table. There's laundry and grocery shopping—and I need to find time to go on a date with Buck. The list is endless…

But in this exact moment in time…I'm not needed. I can just be.

I pick my way across the room and curl up in my bed. I grab a pillow and hug it as I nestle into a ball and close my eyes. I suck a breath in through my nose and slowly let it out through parted lips.

This is my favorite part of the day. When I sit in my room, away from the world and other people. I feel like I can spend hours—maybe even days—up here sleeping.

The lamp on my bedside table flickers. The buzz of electricity creeps into my ears, and I open my eyes. There's a sudden zap, and I'm cast into darkness as the power blows. I scoff. *If he's testing that stupid machine again already…* The air around me is muggy and warm, but I feel a faint breeze tickle my nose. I sit up.

"Dad?" I call out. The dark room doesn't answer. The hair on my arms rises.

A burst of electric, white-hot light flashes across my vision, lighting up the room as if lightning struck right outside my bedroom. But there's no sound—no boom of thunder—and it's gone just as quickly as it came. I scramble to my feet, balancing on the top of my bed. I scan my bedroom. My heart beats against my chest. I wobble and stick my arms out for balance, feet sinking into the soft mattress.

"Dad! If you're testing that stupid—" I step forward, my foot catches on my blanket, and I fall. I bounce off the edge of the bed and thud onto the floor. A box digs into my hip. I slap my hair out of my eyes and struggle to my feet. My breath catches in my throat.

Hovering in the middle of my room, three feet in the air, is an electric blue orb. Swirling arches of electricity crackle off it, like the ocean crashing against a breakwater. It flows and bends and churns in the air, swirling in circles. Wind picks up around me. Waves of heat waft from the dangling ball of light as it swells. The wind rushes faster. I'm pulled an inch toward the orb and grab the side of my bed to steady myself.

Just as quickly as the chaos had started, everything snaps back to normal. Papers fall, the lights flick on, and the orb ejects something big and heavy onto the center of my floor—and then the orb vanishes.

I peer to the floor to see what dropped. It's a figure—a *human* figure. *There's a whole person in the middle of my room.* My eyes dart to the business cards from Miller, which are now strewn all over the place—then I snatch the lamp off my bedside table. I hoist it above my head and step toward the figure on the floor.

"Ow!" it groans. I realize it's a young girl. She pushes herself up on her elbows. I stare at her, eying her inky black hair—it's cut short, just below her chin. It's...*just a kid*. I shake my head and hold the lamp higher.

"How did you get in here?" I demand. I step around the bed. Then, my lip curling, I mutter, "*Where are your parents?*"

The girl—eleven, thirteen at the oldest—looks up at me, her mouth parted into a small "o" shape. There's something familiar about her face, like I've seen it somewhere before. Like when you have a dream about a person you think you know, only to wake up and realize you didn't know them at all.

"Holy-moly—*it actually worked*," the girl whispers, mouth hanging open. A missing tooth leaves a gaping hole in the right side of her smile. Freckles are splattered across her round cheeks. Her eyes are red-rimmed as if she's been crying, and the sight of them strikes me as familiar. How often had I stared into my own red-rimmed eyes in the reflection?

The girl looks around, eyebrows scrunched together. She turns to me, a frown contorting her face. "I mean—I think it worked. You *are* Lorrie, aren't you?"

My eye twitches. "My *name* is *Lorraine*."

The girl snorts. Rolls her eyes. "Okay, yeah, *sure*." She sticks out her hand. "Well, *Lorraine*. Pleased to meet you. My name's Lorrie."

Six

WHEN I WAS A KID, everybody called me Lorrie. I thought my name sounded too "grown up" or something, so I'd refuse to answer to anything other than "Lorrie." But once my mom died and I got a little bit older, "Lorrie" felt too childish. Too *innocent*. So, back to Lorraine it was. People still have a hard time calling me Lorraine. I've been in the same small town my whole life. The people here don't tend to like change very much, no matter if it's a house getting a new coat of paint or a husband getting a new wife. Change causes strife. Words are used as weapons, critiquing and condemning the change. Whispers and rumors, and *Well, you didn't hear this from me's* are exchanged like they're currency. Then ultimately, something *else* changes and everyone's attentions are diverted. They go back to pretending that everything is the same as it once was, even when it isn't and it never will be again. Such is life.

And it really won't be normal again—not with this strange, obtrusive *child* standing three feet away from me. She's wearing low-rise skinny jeans, and a black shirt with pink block letters across the front that say "Justice." Each arm is adorned with a few brightly colored bracelets. She's got obnoxiously spiky pink and green clip-on earrings dangling from her ears. I'd owned a pair just like them when I was a kid—they'd been a gift from Mom to me for my tenth birthday. I inhale sharply.

The girl, "*Lorrie*," spins around in a circle, almost like she's taking in the room around her.

"Whoa," she whispers, then spins back to face me. "We get *tall*."

I keep the lamp above my head. "Listen, *kid*, I don't know who you are or how you got here but you need to get out of my room. *Now*."

Lorrie crosses her arms across her chest. "Hey—this is a lot for me to take in too, you know. I mean, I know our parents *invented* time travel, so I shouldn't be *too* surprised, but come on! I didn't think it'd *actually* work." She looks around the room again. This time her nose wrinkles and she mutters, "Our room is a *mess*."

And then it hits me like a dodgeball to the face. There's a dang good reason why this kid seems so familiar—why I feel like I've met her a long time ago but can't exactly place where.

The kid is me.

I stumble back and let the lamp crash to the floor. I watch as the kid picks her way through the room, grabbing stuff, inspecting it, then tossing it aside.

She picks up an old bra, and her eyes widen. "Ha! Now that is *really* good news!" She giggles, then throws it onto the bed.

I wince, my head spinning. A sharp pain shoots from the base of my neck to my right temple. "This—*no*—this is impossible, this—" I press my palms against my forehead.

Lorrie looks up and frowns. Then she darts across the room and hugs me. She nestles her head into my stomach, squeezing me tight, then takes a step back.

I swallow thickly. "You're—no, you can't be me from the past, that's impossible. I'd remember this."

Lorrie's eyes narrow. "What do you mean? You don't remember this?!"

"No." I cross my arms. Lorrie rolls her eyes and sits on the edge of the bed. "I don't remember this," I continue, "so if it's some sort of prank—"

"But *you're* the one who sent me those videos!" Lorrie cries. "The thumb drive that tells me what to do!"

My gut drops. "How do you know about those?"

Lorrie huffs. "Because you sent them to me."

"That's impossible! I didn't—" I snap my mouth shut. The test Dad had just run on the Machine...my box...but—I thought it had been destroyed! I shake my head at Lorrie. "Okay then, tell me about them. Tell me something specific you remember from the videos."

Lorrie rolls her eyes and flops backwards on the bed. "Well, for starters, you really don't care what you look like. I mean, come on—we're going to *art* school. Everyone knows you can't be ugly at art school. You should brush your hair more—it's always messy in the videos. The ones I watched, at least. I haven't gotten through them all."

I feel my gut twist. Being an artist had been a childhood dream—I'd even gone as far as researching all the top schools. But freshmen year of high school kicked my butt and I started failing all my classes. So, I gave up on art school. If I couldn't even manage high school, clearly college wasn't an option.

"What else?" I ask.

Lorrie kicks her legs and holds up her fingers as she counts off a list. "You lose Bean, our stuffed tiger—I won't forgive you for that, by the way. You threw up at your first high school party, but it was dark so nobody saw and you swore you'd take that secret to your grave. You have a *massive* crush on some guy and you refused to say his name because *what if someone else found your videos*—smart decision, might I add—but anyway, his code name is *Deer* and you really like his butt—"

"I get it." I pinch the bridge of my nose. *Dad is going to lose his mind. The implications of this hurts my brain...* I lean against my dresser. "Why don't I remember coming to the future? If you're here, and you're me...why can't I remember this?"

Smart or not, I've understood a *tiny* fraction of my father's ramblings through the years. I think just being thoroughly steeped in it day in and day out will do that to you—whether you like it or not. Anyway, I knew there could be three different results from being able to travel through time. In theory, that is.

Lorrie sits up and taps her chin. "What do you mean?"

"I mean there are three different outcomes when you travel through time, not including paradoxes. You can either try to change things and accidentally fulfill them, change things and completely *ruin* your future, or change things and create, like, an alternate timeline. Which one are we in?"

Lorrie taps her chin. "Probably the alternate timeline one," she states matter-of-factly. "That happens in the movies, right?"

"You're basing your understanding of time travel off of movies?" I frown. "Dad says time travel is—"

"Dad doesn't know his left hand from his right hand!" Lorrie spits. "I know what we have to do, anyway. And if you hadn't sent your videos back, I'd never have watched them, and we'd never be having this conversation! You changed the past with those videos! And if you were able to bring me here, think of all the other stuff we could change!"

I raise a single brow. "Like what?"

Lorrie leans forward. There's a spark in her eyes—*is it excitement? Hope?* She whispers, "We can save Mom."

The lump lodges back in my throat.

Lorrie continues. "Don't you see? We can go back—you and me, *together*—and we can stop her from stepping into the Machine! Stop Dad from even turning it on!"

My skull feels too small for my aching brain. I shake it my head. "But—you and I...you shouldn't even be here. This whole thing is a paradox."

"Oh my gosh—get with the program already! I gave you a hug, didn't I? There wasn't any black hole, or—or time fizzling out of existence. Nothing bad has happened!"

I clench my jaw. She's right, as far as I can tell. None of Dad's warnings have happened. I press my palms to my forehead and try to breathe.

"This shouldn't be possible—this *can't* be possible," I whisper.

"Look—" Lorrie unzips the small, panda-head-shaped bag

on her hip and pulls out a stuffed tiger. "I can prove who I am—I brought Bean!"

She tosses me the tiger and I catch it with both hands. I roll him over and inspect him, going right to the name tag. When I'd scrawled my initials on it with black Sharpie, the ink had bled into the fabric, making the letters big and puffy with tiny black veins shooting out. I'd hated how it'd looked as a kid and had hidden Bean in my bed for ages out of shame. But now I hold him gently in my hands, his fur just as soft as the day I'd lost him.

"Holy—" I held a hand over my mouth as reality crashed in. "Oh my gosh—you're *me*—you're *really* me."

Lorrie grins and sits up straighter. I look from Bean to her small, round face. My head spins, I stumble back, and the world around me turns black.

I awake to water splashing across my face. I splutter and bolt upright. Above me, Lorrie casually screws the top of my water bottle back on and chucks it onto the bed.

"You know, I would have hoped we'd handle life a little better in the future." Lorrie sits on the ground next to me. "Just don't pass out when we go back to save Mom, m'kay?"

"Save Mom?" I wipe my face off with my sleeve and look at her. "We can't save Mom—you know that we're not supposed to change anything with time travel, just observe."

Lorrie sags back, her eyes rolling into her head. "Ugh, you sound like Dad!"

"Hey! No, I don't!"

"Do too." She sticks her tongue out and crosses her arms. "Listen—if I took the time to explain everything about this to you, we'd be here for hours. And we hate science and math and—" she stops, her eyes narrowing. "Wait, do you like science now?"

I shake my head, and she lets out a breath of relief.

"Oh, thank God. Anyway, I'm not going to bother with it. Do you want to save Mom or not?"

I clench my teeth, and a fresh pressure builds behind my eyes. I stare at Lorrie, so young and hurt, her wounds so fresh. "I..."

A knock at my door.

"Lorraine?" my dad calls. Lorrie and I look at each other, eyes wide. She squeezes her eyes shut, puffs out her cheeks, and vanishes in a zap of electricity just as the door starts to creak open. I stand and dust off my jeans as my dad pokes his head through my door.

"Yeah?" I ask. My voice is thick. I clear my throat.

"I, uh...I brought you spaghetti." Dad holds out a bowl of

pasta. I can smell the Italian seasoning and spicy sausage. I let my shoulders deflate.

"Thanks," I whisper and sit on my bed. Dad grins and pushes the door open further. He steps inside and picks his way through my room, careful not to step on any of my belongings. He sits next to me and passes me the bowl. I stare at the noodles and twirl them with the fork, then I look up at him. My words pass through my lips like air leaking from a tire. "Can you tell me about Mom?"

I can tell the question alone hurts him. He immediately stares at his hands clasped in his lap. His eyebrows scrunch together in the middle, reminding me of a caterpillar inching across his wrinkled forehead.

"Of course," he finally whispers. "What do you want to know?"

A frown tugs at my lips. My heart hammers in my chest and my intestines wriggle together like a bowl of worms. I don't know why the question popped from my mouth—my head's still reeling. *Time travel is possible.* What else is possible? What else should be possible?

"What did she want?" I ask, focusing on the old candy wrapper hidden on my floor halfway under a discarded sneaker. "Like—most in the world...what did she want most in the world? She was a scientist—a time travel specialist. She'd have to have had big aspirations, right?"

My dad rubs his scruffy jaw with his hand and stares up at the ceiling.

"You." He looks at me and tries to smile. The edges of his lips waver. "She wanted to know you. Family was the most important thing to her—to both of us. She wanted us to be together. You see...your mom...she came from a broken home. Her parents fought a lot and...she got, well...she got caught in the crossfire sometimes."

I shift. My mattress squeaks under me. My dad puts his hand on my shoulder, and the weight in my gut twists like a knife.

"Family is the most important thing, Lorraine. We... I know we don't always get along, but...well, I'm trying, and...I know you are too." He squeezes my shoulder, and I briefly look up from the floor to meet his eyes. His earnest, pathetic eyes. What would he do if I told him? Told him right now? I look back down at the floor. The floor doesn't scrutinize me with its gaze. It doesn't promise me things it can't do.

Dad continues, "I want you to know, Lorraine...I would do anything possible to keep this family together and...well, I'd hope you'd do the same."

I nod and slowly twirl the spaghetti on the fork, watching the noodles flop helplessly. I'm not hungry but I slowly bring it to my mouth and take a bite anyway.

Huh… Family is the most important thing? For a moment, I can feel my heart warm at the thought. But then I think of that stupid Machine downstairs—of today and all the days before it—and I feel the sentiment leave like a candle getting snuffed.

"Thanks, Dad, for the pasta." I hold up the bowl. "I'm… pretty tired, so…I think I'm going to bed."

My dad smiles, squeezes my shoulder one last time, then stands and makes his way to the door. "Goodnight, Lorraine. Sleep well, I love you, see you in the morning."

I give a tight response: "Yep, see you in the morning."

The door shuts…

I know what I have to do.

The only one who can bridge the gap between Dad and me is the only one who was able to do it before.

"Okay," I say to the empty room. I set the bowl on my bed-side table and scramble around my room. I gather clothes and change into a new outfit—jeans and a black *Imagine Dragons* T-shirt. I slip on my tennis shoes and stand in the middle of my room. "Okay!" I say again. Silence ticks by. My cheeks heat for a second. I'm speaking to *nothing*. But how else am I supposed to tell Lorrie I'm ready?

Third time's the charm. "Okay, I'm ready…I…I said I'm ready…hello?"

Nope. Silence.

I look around, trying to catch sight of any strange lights or weird electric waves. The only thing I see is Bean, the tiny stuffed tiger Lorrie'd left behind, staring back at me from the bed.

Seven

I LEAN AGAINST THE GRUBBY KFC COUNTER and try desperately to keep a smile on my face. People mill about, their chatter clanging together like a choir where everyone has different sheets of music to play off of.

It's been about a week since I met my past self, and at this point I'm beginning to think it was a crazy, grief-fueled dream. The only thing keeping me from thinking I'm crazy is the stuffed tiger on my bed. She'd left him behind. My stomach knots just thinking about it—because technically *I* left it there, and if I left it there, does that mean that's why I lost it? Was it even *me*? Because, like, Lorrie is me, but she's also *not* me if she's from a parallel timeline. So, if she lost her Bean in my world, then where did I lose my Bean? Ugh. My brain hurts just thinking about it. It doesn't make sense.

I sigh. I stretch my back as a group of obnoxiously lively

teenagers pile into the store and hover by the register. I watch as they whisper together, glancing my way before bursting into giggles. *What's their problem?*

"Lorraine!" Barb shouts from the back, and I instinctively straighten.

"Yeah?" I turn to look at her, and my smile drops. Miller stands behind her, his face grim like his name's Severus Snape.

"The police want to talk to you," Barb says carefully, her eyes warily staring at me. I flash a grin and walk past them to the back.

"This will only take a minute," Miller assures Barb as he follows after me. He escorts me past Charlie, past the freezer, then finally stops by the large metal racks of supplies.

The second we're alone, I cross my arms and turn to him. "How *dare* you come to my boss, lie about who—"

"Miss Lorraine, has your father run an illegal experiment with Huson-sanctioned ideas and lab equipment?" Miller steps forward. I take a half-step back.

I swallow and try not to let the rush of anxiety show on my face. "What makes you think that?" I ask carefully.

"Lorraine, I've been kind to you up until this point. I've only waited for you where your coworkers and boss won't see. I've kept our visits to *once* a week and made them brief for your benefit. Listen to me when I say this…" He leans forward and takes off his sunglasses. He stares me directly in the eyes, and for some reason I find those brown orbs far more intimidating than the dark shades from before. He continues softly, just above the hum of the air conditioner, "If we suspect that your father is continuing with his scientific research, we will not hesitate to take immediate and dramatic action against him, you, and any other persons or items that stand in our way. Do I make myself clear?"

I scoff. "You know, you seem to take your job with Huson Labs real serious. Maybe you need a vacation day."

Miller's lip twitches up and I think for just a second that he might smile. "You think I work *for* Huson Laboratories?"

Those words send an icy chill down my spine. "Don't you?"

"You're foolish and naive, Lorraine. You have no idea the sort of people who are…*interested* in this." He doesn't break eye contact as he speaks, his words precise and crisp. "Do I make myself clear?" he repeats.

I nod.

"Good. Now, has your father started his research again?"

"No, sir," I whisper. My heart hammers in my chest. "He hasn't."

I mean…he never stopped his research, so how could he start it again?

Mr. Miller leans back. He stares at me with a grizzly frown, squinting as his eyes dance over my face. I clench my fist and dawn the oh-so-practiced customer service smile that I've used every day since I started working here.

"Can I help you with anything else?" I ask. Then, I cross my arms and add, "Or are you done bothering me?"

"I think you're lying to me, Lorraine," Miller says, ignoring my threats. He smooths down his tie and slowly puts his glasses back on. "There's something different about you today. You're hiding something."

"I'm an open book, *Agent* Miller." I roll my eyes. "Mom's dead, Dad's never recovered from the grief, and I'm just trying to save up enough money to get out of here. What more do you need to know?"

Miller scoffs. He turns toward the back exit, then pauses before leaving and says, "I'll be in touch."

"And I'll be here like always because *nothing has changed!*" I call after him as the big gray door shuts with a clang. I let out a breath and lean against the metal shelving unit. I press my forehead against the cold pole of the shelves and close my eyes. Now that he's gone, I can feel my legs trembling. Does he know about Lorrie? No, how could he? I barely know about Lorrie.

"Lorraine!" Barb yells from the front. "We got customers!"

I suck in a breath and press my palms against my forehead. I splash cool water over my face from the sink, wipe my face off with the bottom of my shirt, and then step out of the back and up to the register.

"Sorry, Barb!" I call as she saunters to the back, already reaching for her pack of cigarettes. She hates being in the front—dealing with the customers and taking orders *"exhausts her,"* or so she says. I wonder why she bothers to own this KFC if she hates it so much.

"Sorry about the wait—what can I get started for you today?" I ask.

"A huge bucket of drumsticks—hey, it's a good thing KFC hasn't changed much since you were a kid, right?"

My heart drops and I look up from the register.

Little me—Lorrie—stands on the other side of the counter with a massive grin. She glances toward the back and leans close. Her hands cup the side of her mouth as she whispers, "I don't have any money, though. Think you can cover me?"

I grip the sides of the monitor and hiss, "*What* are you *doing* here?!"

"You never gave me an answer on if we were going to save Mom—"

I grab her wrist and look toward the entrance on the right.

Miller's car—the silver sedan—is still parked out front. He hasn't left yet—*why hasn't he left yet?*

"Ow—*ow*!" Lorrie tries to wrestle free.

"You don't understand—you can't be here!" I snap. "We're in *danger*."

Lorrie stops and scans the KFC. "Why? Is Dad here?"

"What? No—Miller—I mean, the lab Dad worked for—*works* for!" I suck in a breath. What am I thinking? Does she already know about Dad being fired? What does she know about her future? *What is she even doing here?* I reach into my pocket and pull out my phone. I type out a text, still holding Lorrie's wrist with my other hand.

"Who are you texting? Woah—that phone is *so* shiny! When do we finally get a phone?" Lorrie leans forward again, and I move the phone so she can't see what I'm typing.

"My boyfriend," I say. "And no, I'm not telling you who it is—you shouldn't even know that I *have* a boyfriend."

Emergency. Come get me ASAP.

I send the message and slip the phone back into my pocket. I look up at Lorrie. Her cheeks are tinted red, her eyes wide, and her mouth hanging open like a giant grouper fish.

"What?" I ask.

"Boyfriend?" Her voice is high-pitched. It reminds me of a piglet squealing.

"Shh!" I quickly glance to the back. "Keep your voice down!"

"Is it Josh Hutcherson?!" Lorrie asks.

I turn back to her, aghast. "What? No—we live in the middle of *nowhere* in *Ohio*! Get a hold of yourself."

People are starting to stare. The couple at the table on our left keeps glancing over, so I flash them a quick smile.

I snap my gaze back to Lorrie and scowl. "You're coming with me—we have to get you out of here."

"Righto!" She finally wrestles her wrist free from my grip. "But I'm starving, so you better get me those drumsticks before we go—oh! And a side of mashed potatoes! I love the mashed potatoes here."

"Not once you find out how they're made," I mutter. I grab a large cup and glance to the back again. I'm not *technically* allowed any free drinks. They come out of my paycheck—if I'm caught. But...technically...this isn't *me* drinking them. Lorrie doesn't work at KFC. I look at the little girl who is standing in front of me.

"7UP—no ice," she says. I nod, fill the cup, and pass her the drink. My phone dings, and I pull it out of my pocket, glancing at the message.

OMW. R U OK???

A sigh of relief escapes my lips. Buck is good like this—ready to drop whatever it is he's doing to help.

Lorrie leans against the counter, her eyes shining. "Does he at least *look* like Josh Hutcherson?" she asks, wiggling her eyebrows.

I think for a second, then frown. "Think...more like Dylan O'Brien," I say, "but not with a beard. Think, like, his Teen Wolf era."

Lorrie's face falls. "Oh," she whispers. Then, after a second, says, "I don't know who that is."

I pause for just a moment. *When had I gotten into that show?* I shake my head. That doesn't matter right now.

"Stay here," I command, then I run to the back and grab a bucket. I fill it with as many drumsticks as I can, then dash to the front. "Hold this."

Lorrie's eyes widen as she accepts the bucket.

I unclip my name tag, swipe off my hat, and jump over the counter. "We need to get—"

"Lorraine!" Barb shouts from the back. She bustles forward, a scowl contorting her features. "Where do you think you're going?"

"I—" I exhale sharply. "She—family emergency, Barb! I'm sorry! I'll take an extra shift next week—swear!"

"No! No, no, that's not how *a job* works, Lorraine. You don't get to leave a shift whenever you—" Barbara snaps her mouth shut as Lorrie stalks up to her with a glare.

Lorrie holds her fingers to her forehead as she sneers. "What. *Ever*. Major. Loser!" Her fingers shape a W, E, M, and L as she speaks.

I pinch the bridge of my nose and fight the urge to grab Lorrie and shove her where no one would ever be able to find her again. I think she'd thrive in Gollum's cave... Barb, for her part, is at a loss for words. She stares, her mouth half open, eyes wide, and that vein in her forehead twitching like a half-smooshed bug. Lorrie grins and bounces back to me.

"What was that?" I complain.

Lorrie grabs my hand and pulls me toward the door. "She was being so rude," Lorrie whines, "I had to put her in her place!" We step into the muggy afternoon air. "Why didn't you tell her off? She shouldn't talk to you like that."

I let go of Lorrie's hand and cross my arms.

I'd forgotten how...*atrocious* I'd been as a kid. Antagonistic. Spiteful. When had I lost that audacity? That ability to put a person in their place and step up for what I believe in? I remember, when I was a kid, my dad and I would go toe to toe over the stupidest, pettiest things.

"So, where's our car?" Lorrie scans the parking lot. She points to the silver sedan and my stomach clenches. "That one? It's so shiny!"

I slap her hand and glance around. I don't see Miller, but the hair on the back of my neck rises. I feel like I'm being watched. I suck in a breath and cross my arms tight over my stomach as I wait for the familiar blue pickup truck.

"I don't have a car," I finally say. "Buck is picking us up."

Lorrie's nose scrunches. "Buck?" she asks, her words dripping with disgust. I look down and quirk an eyebrow.

"Yes, Buck—that's my boyfriend."

"*Our* boyfriend." Lorrie corrects as she pulls out a drumstick and begins to munch.

My eyebrows shoot up. "No, no—*my* boyfriend. You are a *child*," I snap. "And why didn't you grab any napkins?"

"Well..." Lorrie swallows a mouthful of chicken. She motions to me with her drumstick. "No matter what he is, he can't know about me."

"What?" I ask. "Why not?"

"Think about the mess that would make," Lorrie laughs. "You're the only one who can know, because...the timeline needs to remain intact!"

I cross my arms. "The timeline's already messed up. Telling one more person isn't going to change anything."

Lorrie glances at me from the corner of her eye. Her eyebrows draw together, and her lips pull into a half-pout-half-frown.

"Whatever. Just don't tell him. Drumstick?" She holds out a greasy chicken piece.

I scowl, nose scrunching. "Hard pass," I mutter.

I scan the parking lot again. It's only three and a half more anxiety-inducing minutes before the familiar pickup squeals into the parking lot. The engine revs, then the truck barrels toward us. It screeches to a halt at the curb.

"*That's* Buck?" Lorrie asks. Her nose scrunches as she looks up at me, then back to Buck as he jumps from the truck and rushes around the front. "Hard pass."

"Lorraine—are you okay? What's going on?" Buck asks as he scoops me into a hug. I close my eyes and let the scent of fresh dirt waft over me before I pull back. *He must've been helping his family work the field...*

I ignore the twist of guilt in my abdomen and push Buck toward his truck. "We gotta go—Miller's poking around."

He grabs my hand and grins. "Say no more!" He opens the passenger door for me, quirking an eyebrow as Lorrie bounds in and settles into the middle seat.

"Uh...who's the kid?" He jabs a thumb toward her. She glares at him and sticks out her tongue—bits of fried chicken coat it.

Somewhere deep, *deep* inside, I feel the urge to bury myself in a hole and never come out. I pinch the bridge of my nose. Lorrie is right. This is going to get complicated.

"I'll explain on the way home," I sigh, scooting into the passenger seat. Buck walks around the truck, climbs in, and stares at Lorrie. She stares back, her face drawn into a neutral expression.

She points to his face. "You got chocolate on your lip."

Buck's eyes widen, and he glances at me. "It's not chocolate. It's a mole," he says. He sticks his hand out toward Lorrie. "My name's Buck, by the way. What's your—"

"*For the love of God,* would you just *drive?!*" I cry.

Buck flinches, then shifts into drive and shakes his head. The truck rumbles, a deep, unsettling vibration that jostles my bones. As we speed out of the parking lot, Lorrie gasps and clutches her seatbelt. I grab the handle of the door—the plastic rattling in my grip—as we swerve onto the highway and race toward the terrible unknown.

Eight

MY FOOT BOUNCES UP AND DOWN as we barrel down the freeway. I keep glancing into the side mirror. I shift, craning my neck to stare out the back window. I can't see Miller's car anywhere, but I can't shake the feeling that we're being followed. It feels like, I don't know—like someone's standing just behind me, breathing on my neck. It tickles my hair, sends a shiver down my spine, and yet every time I jump and flip around, there's no one there.

I force a breath out of my mouth and glance at Buck. He's gripping the steering wheel, staring straight ahead with his jaw clenched. I swallow and look at my lap. Lorrie sits between us, content. She's swaying from side to side, munching on her drumsticks.

"Are you going to tell me what's going on?" Buck finally asks.

I huff. "Miller came into work today—hauled me to the back

like I was some *child* being pulled out of class for misbehaving. I just... I couldn't stay after that."

Buck's mouth drops open. "What? Why would he do that?"

"*Because* he's sure I'm hiding something about—" I stop and look down at Lorrie. She's got her big, dark eyes trained on me. I clear my throat and hold out my hand. She passes me a drumstick.

I motion to Lorrie with the chicken leg. "Buck, this is Lorrie."

"I'm Lorraine's little cousin, pleased to meet—*ow*!" She stops as I flick the side of her head.

"She's me—from the past. Dad's machine worked."

For a moment, we swerve between the lanes. I grip the door. Lorrie clutches the bucket of drumsticks to her chest. Buck hisses a curse, then settles back into his lane. He keeps driving, eyes wide. I watch as he swallows then nods his head. He clicks on the turn signal and moves toward an off-ramp.

"Buck?" I ask. He keeps silent until we pull off the ramp and park on the side of the road. Then he gets out and lets the door slam behind him. The whole car rattles, the sound echoing in my ears.

"Uh, is he good?" Lorrie asks.

I unbuckle and slip out of the truck. "Stay here," I order, hurling the door shut behind me. I jog around to the front of the truck. I wrap my arms around my middle, squeezing my abdomen as I slowly slink up to Buck. He's got his hands on his hips and is staring off into the sky, his eyebrows drawn tightly together.

"Buck?" I lick my lips, eyes darting to the highway. I shake my head. "Buck, you okay?"

He looks at me—his eyes drilling into my very heart. "Are you messing with me?" His voice is low—deadly serious.

"Messing with you? You think I'd lie about something like this?" I snap.

Buck shakes his head. "You get this once, okay? One time, you get to tell me time travel is real, and no matter what I'll believe you. But if this is a prank or a joke—"

"It's real." I glower and mutter, "I wouldn't joke about something like this, Buck, *you know that.*"

"You're right, babe, I'm sorry."

Then he's hugging me. I can feel him rest his head against my own.

"Time travel—holy cow, your dad invented time travel," he whispers. The tension in my shoulder bleeds out for just a moment—but then a truck backfires somewhere on the freeway, and I jolt. I pull back to scan the road.

"Miller *knows* something's up," I whisper. "I-I don't know

how, but things *changed* today. Why else, except for him knowing something about Lorrie? We can't stay here."

Buck pulls back and looks up the road. He nods, rubbing a
circle on my shoulder. "Right. Well, let's get you back to your
dad's, then."

A loud knock comes from inside the truck. We look, and I
can see Lorrie scowling.

"You tell Dad and I'll hit you!" she shouts. She scoots to the
driver's seat and rolls down the window. She sticks her head out
and glares, eyes hard and cold—well, as hard and cold as a little
girl's glare can be. "I'm serious—he *can't* know."

"Why?" Buck demands. "This is *his* research!"

Lorrie grabs her hair and pulls. "He just can't! It'd ruin
everything!"

I sigh and press my palms against my forehead.

"Babe, she can't be serious," Buck whispers.

I take a step away and groan. "I don't know—*I don't know!*"
I smooth my hair back. I bite my lip and look at Lorrie. "I... You
know how he's like—he wouldn't understand."

"Wouldn't understand?" Buck repeats. He throws his arms in
the air. "Your dad, the *inventor* of *time travel*, wouldn't understand this?!"

"We're trying to save Mom," I snap. Buck's arms fall to his

sides, mouth parted. My heart begins to beat heavier and harder in my chest, and I find words spilling from my mouth before I can stop them. "We could do it—Dad said that Mom wanted us to all stay together! Besides, if Dad *wasn't* trying to fix his mistake, then why's he been continuing his research this whole time, huh? I-I mean, come on! *This*? This *has* to be the reason he's been so obsessive." I square my shoulders and jut out my jaw. "Family is the most important thing," I say—and even as I say it, I can't help but cringe. "I... Buck, we need your help."

Buck rubs the back of his neck and stares at the ground. I'm left listening to the rumble of the truck engine and the cars zooming by on the highway. I take another glance at the road. My throat closes for a moment as I spot a silver sedan on the off-ramp. My stomach drops. I take a step back.

It drives by, a woman in her late seventies in the driver's seat. I let out a breath and, shakily, focus back on Buck.

Finally, he looks me in the eye. "Your Dad needs to know," he whispers. I can see Lorrie straining out the window to try and hear. Buck takes a step toward me and wraps me in another hug. "You know he does, Lorraine. I-I mean, those rules he has are pretty clear. Don't pretend to be God? Walk through time like you walk through a national park?"

"Technically *we* aren't breaking any of those rules," I say.

"I mean, I haven't done any time traveling. *Lorrie's* the one breaking them."

Buck frowns and looks me in the eye.

"*Eventually*," I promise. "I-I swear, I'll tell him about it— *soon*... Just...just give Lorrie and me some time to figure this out, kay?"

"M'kay," Buck whispers, then presses a kiss to the top of my head.

The horn blares, and we both jump. Lorrie is lying on the wheel, scowling.

"Stop that!" I snarl. She relents, sinking back in the seat, grumbling under her breath. I huff as Buck shakes his head.

"Does feeding your past self chicken count as disrespecting the wildlife?" he asks. I flick his arm. He chuckles, rubbing the spot where I got him. When he jogs away, I let out a breath—take one final look at the highway—and get back in the truck.

"So, what's the plan?" Buck asks. Lorrie holds out her empty bucket of drumsticks.

"More chicken!" she cheers.

"No!" I snap. "You've had more than enough. We need a place to go—somewhere that isn't home. Dad's going to be there—on the porch, blabbering on the phone—and if he catches even a *glance* at Lorrie, he'll know."

Lorrie rolls her eyes and mutters, "If he's not too busy with *work*, you mean…"

Apparently, my angst had started young.

Buck buckles his seat, shifts into drive, and we peel off toward the freeway. Lorrie continues to grumble under her breath. I reach into the bucket, pull out some chicken, and bring it to my mouth. But my stomach clenches as I think about the child sitting next to me—about the possibilities, the risks—and I let the chicken fall from my fingers and tumble back into the bucket.

Nine

WE RUMBLE DOWN THE DIRT ROAD, tall rows of corn on either side of the truck. Lorrie watches the fields, her eyes wide. Buck lives in the *middle* of the middle of nowhere, on his parents' farm. His folks are hard-working individuals who'd inherited the farm from Buck's grandfather, whom we all lovingly call Papa. He'd started the farm with nothing but a barren field and three corn seeds in his pocket—or so the story goes.

Papa had wanted corn to be the family business, for his sons and for his sons' sons. That included Buck, who found his passions lie more in the *computer* sciences rather than the *agricultural* sciences. Buck and my dad can talk for hours about theories I really couldn't care less about—and when they'd first met, they had. My dad had encouraged Buck to pursue his own career and had gifted him one of his old laptops, which Papa hadn't taken kindly to. To keep the peace (and his new laptop),

Buck had opted to move into the tiny, run-down trailer in the middle of their property instead of the family farmhouse.

Buck and I don't mind too much. It's nice to have a place away from it all, so to speak, even if there is the occasional cockroach.

Lorrie, however, seems to have a different perspective. As we come around the bend, down to the end of the road, and in front of the trailer underneath the oak tree, she gasps and recoils in her seat.

"Tell me that's not where you live," she whispers.

Buck glares. "What's wrong with it?" he demands, pulling up to the tree and slamming on the brakes. We all three lurch forward, then lurch back into our seats as Buck shifts into park.

"Hmm? Nothing! Nothing at all, *Buck*." Lorrie spits his name as if it's a gristly bite of chicken, stringy and grainy against her tongue. She's still got grease and fried crumbs around her mouth, and I grimace. Buck sucks in a breath, shakes his head, and climbs out of the truck. The moment the door shuts, Lorrie's got a finger in her mouth, pretending to gag.

I slap her hand and scowl. "Don't be rude!"

Lorrie mutters a string of words I hadn't realized I'd known at that age as we slip out of the truck. We follow Buck up the rickety porch steps (the ones he'd built all by himself) and wait in the waning sunlight as he fishes his keys out of his jeans and unlocks the door.

If Lorrie was unimpressed with the outside, I can only imagine what she must be thinking about the inside. I haven't been over in a little under a month—which seems to be the last time Buck has cleaned. Clothes litter the floor and dishes clog the sink.

"Well, make yourself at home." Buck motions to the two beanbags on the ground, facing a flat-screen TV.

"You see that TV?" I lean down to Lorrie's height and point. "Buck saved that from a dumpster. He got it to work, all on his own. Impressive, right?"

Lorrie gives me an unimpressed side-eye. I frown. *Whatever.* She doesn't have to like him. *I* like him, and that's what matters.

Lorrie scrunches her nose and watches as Buck goes to the bedroom, which is nestled in the back of the trailer like a janitor's closet. The moment his figure disappears inside, Lorrie hurriedly turns to me.

"Don't worry," she whispers. "I'll fix this. You won't have to date him for much longer."

I huff and cross my arms. "Lorrie, despite what you might think, I actually *really* like Buck."

She recoils. "Why?!"

"He's..." I thought about it for a second. His charming eyes. His strong hands. How he holds me when I'm crying. "Reliable," I finally say.

"If you wanted reliable, you should've asked for a dog," Lorrie mutters. She crosses her arms, stalks over to the beanbag, and sits. "I should have listened to Abby Johnson—she had me play MASH the other day, and it said I'd live in a shack!"

I threw my hands in the air. "I don't *live* here!"

Lorrie looks up and huffs a single strand of black hair out of her round face. "But if you get *married,* you *will.*" She stresses each word as if I'm an idiot. Then, in a grumble, she adds, "Besides, he doesn't look anything like Josh Hutcherson."

"Hey," Buck calls as he emerges from his bedroom, "I don't think I have much food left, but I've got some Kraft Mac & Cheese!" He shakes the blue box in his hand and grins.

"You keep food in your room?" Lorrie asks.

The place is tiny, *okay?* And what cabinet space his kitchen *does* have is reserved for dishes. His so-called "pantry" is a little shelf in the corner of his room—that's all he's got space for. And I'm about to explain all of this to Lorrie but Buck swoops in before I can.

"I'll make it with extra butter and milk to make it soupy, just for you."

My heart flutters in my chest, and I look down at Lorrie. I'd told him months ago that, as a kid, I refused any Mac & Cheese that wasn't Kraft and made with about three times as much milk as the package directed.

I watch as Lorrie's eyes widen. She looks from Buck, back to me. I nod toward him as a grin pulls at my cheeks.

"Well?" I ask. "You want some?"

She crosses her arms. "Only if *you're* having some."

I roll my eyes and walk into the kitchen. I stand on my tip-toes and press a quick kiss against Buck's cheek. "We'll take it. Thanks, babe."

"I can still see you!" Lorrie cries.

Buck clicks his teeth and grins as he mutters, "Wow, you were just a peach, weren't 'cha?"

I pat his arm and slip around him. "It was middle school. Don't tell me you were all cupcakes and rainbows back then."

"I can hear you, too." Lorrie grunts.

I reach under the counter into one of the only cupboards and pull out a pot. The bottom is rusty brown. I blow the dust off and swipe a finger along the inside, grimacing.

"When was the last time you cooked?" I ask as I squeeze around him and stick the pot under the faucet.

"I made chicken nuggets just last night!" he grins. "Aren't you proud of me?"

"Always," I snort. Then we settle into a quiet silence as I set about boiling the water, and he grabs the different ingredients from the fridge. Buck and I work well together, slipping around each other in the small, cramped space. It's like a dance, unchoreographed and full of improvisation. We twist and turn around each other, a hand pressed against a back here, a soft touch on the arm here, alerting each other of intention and presence with barely a word spoken between us. It's beautiful, in its own weird, perfect-for-*me* kind of way.

I can feel Lorrie watching me from her beanbag, her arms crossed and lips pulled tightly together.

I'd been so sure of my life back then—before Mom died. I was dedicated and passionate. Stubborn and defiant. I knew what I wanted out of life, and I wasn't going to let anything or anyone sway me.

But after the accident...I don't know. It must be strange for Buck to see the two of us standing next to each other. She is so different from who I am now. Do we even look like each other? Could an outsider even see the resemblance between us?

Within half an hour, Buck and I have three soupy bowls of Mac & Cheese. We step into the living room. I take the other bean bag and Buck takes the floor. He passes the paper bowl to Lorrie. The moment she has it in her hands, she begins to scarf it down.

"Woah," Buck whispers. "Were you always such a pig with food? That's a whole bowl of cheese and a tub of KFC, if I recall."

Lorrie shakes her head and hastily wipes her chin with her

sleeve. "Nope. Time travel did this—every time I jump, I feel like I'm going to starve. Can I have another bowl?"

I pass her my bowl and watch as she devours it. Finally, she starts to slow. By the time Buck finishes his, Lorrie is reclined in the beanbag, smiling.

"Now then," she claps. "Let's get down to business. If we want to save Mom, you're going to need to figure out how to time travel."

"Can't we just use Dad's machine?" I ask.

"Ew—*no*! You could time travel at my age, so you should be able to now. We don't need Dad."

I look at my white sneakers and pick at the plastic end of the shoelace. "Okay, but I don't remember how to time travel."

"That's the problem," Lorrie drawls. She throws her head back against the beanbag and stares at the ceiling with a frown. "I remember things that you don't—of course, we could chalk that up to old age—"

"I'm only twenty."

"—but no matter the reason," she continues, ignoring me, "our goal is still the same. You gotta figure out how to time travel like me, otherwise there's no way we'll save Mom."

"And how exactly do you plan on saving your mom?" Buck asks.

Lorrie sits up and looks at him. "Why do you care?" she sneers.

I bolt upright. "Listen here, you *little*—" I stop as Buck grabs my hand and squeezes. I look down at our fingers, intertwined, his thumb rubbing the back of my hand.

"It's okay, Lorraine, breathe," he whispers. I take a calming breath in through my nose and let it out through my mouth. I then shoot Lorrie a glare, and she shrugs, putting her hands up in a mock surrender.

"Okay, okay, whatever—you *care*. We'll believe that for now." She stands and claps her hands again. "Right—once you know how to time travel, we can figure out how to save Mom. I have a couple of ideas, but right now that's not important. So—here, stand up!"

I let Lorrie pull me to my feet. Buck stands too, and we face her together.

"Time travel is *really* easy. It's like snapping your fingers." Lorrie grins. "In one moment, you're here—and in the next it's 1995! So go on, snap your fingers and see what happens."

I look at Buck, my eyebrows scrunch together, then slowly look back at Lorrie. "I... That *can't* work."

"Come on, can't you just try?" Lorrie pleads. I cross my arms tight across my chest.

"This feels stupid," I complain. Buck and Lorrie are watching me. I feel a heat rise in my neck.

Buck pats my arm and whispers so only I can hear, "Come on, you can do it. I believe in you."

I throw my head back and my arms down at my side. "*Fine*! Okay, fine, I'll try."

I swallow, hold up my hand, and suck in a breath. Then, I snap.

Surprise, surprise, *nothing happens*! It's stupid to think I would be able to do something that not even my dad—a legit time travel scientist—had managed to figure out how to do in his entire career. *I'm just me.*

"See, I told you this was stupid," I grumble. Lorrie steps forward and grabs my hand. She looks at it and her eyes squint together as she holds up her own hand to compare.

"Hmm... Maybe it's because you're old and your hands are too wrinkly," she whispers. I yank my arm out of her grasp and scoff. She steps back and taps her chin. "Well, if this fails, we could always go to Uncle Seb," she says.

"Why on earth would we go to him?" I grimace.

Lorrie shrugs. "I don't know. I overheard him and Dad talking about one of his new inventions. It's this thing that makes you do whatever someone else wants you to do! I could stick it on you and tell you to time travel!"

A wave of nausea rises from my stomach into my throat. I don't like the implications of what Uncle Sebastian and, in extension, Huson Laboratory were working on.

"Maybe try jumping?" Buck suggests. I shoot him a glare.

"That's not helping," I say. He holds his hands up in surrender.

Lorrie waves her arms beside me. "No—no! He's on to something! I always jump when I travel. Jump in the air and think of a specific moment in the past—like when Mom was in the Machine and—"

"I can't think of that!" I bark. Lorrie's arms fall to her sides, eyes wide. She looks at me like I've just slapped her—and that expression is so familiar, so similar to one I've seen dozens of times—that I can't help what comes out of my mouth next. "*Geeze*, you're acting just like *Dad*."

Her mouth drops, and her hands curl into fists.

"You take that back!" she shouts. She steps toward me. I square my shoulders and step toward her.

"Or what?" I sneer.

Then Buck has his hand on my shoulder, pushing me back. "Whoa, whoa, let's calm down. No fighting in the trailer—house rules."

His words do little to appease us. I turn away stiffly. Lorrie, from behind me, sniffles. I glance over my shoulder. She's got her arm over her eyes, her teeth clenched together.

"Babe...it might help if you explain *why* you can't talk

about it," Buck whispers, his voice a soothing balm on a wound. My throat tightens, and I look to the ground.

"I *can't* remember it." I force the words out through my teeth.

In front of me, Lorrie looks up. "Oh..." she trails off. Then she closes her eyes and turns away. She drums her fingers against the side of her head and lets out a low hum. "Okay, then." She turns back to me. "What's a moment you remember leading up to that?"

I shift and wrap my arms around my middle. "I-I don't know."

"Come on, *Lorraine*," Lorrie drags out my name. "Just think!"

"I told you, I don't—" I stop as a memory comes to mind. We'd gone out to Olive Garden to celebrate something—I can't remember what. All I remember is the dress I had. It'd been my Christmas dress from the year before. The fanciest thing I had owned, with a velvety, black, long-sleeved top that had a huge red bow across the middle, and a Christmas plaid skirt that went down to just below my knees. I remembered how that dress would scratch at my legs, but I didn't care because I felt so pretty in it. I remembered the smell of my mother's perfume. Sweet and thick, like she'd sprayed herself with just a pinch too much.

"Okay..." I nod. "Olive Garden. Right before the accident, we—"

Lorrie jumps in the air, grinning. "To celebrate Dad and

Mom's anniversary! I remember! They took me because I begged and begged. I didn't want to be alone."

I frown. Again, more details I don't remember...but maybe it's not the details that matter. Maybe it's the moments that stick with you. The feelings and the smells.

"Okay," I roll my shoulders. I let that memory play on loop in my mind. "Okay—I'm going to try. I'm going to go back to that moment."

"Okay." Lorrie claps her hands together and takes a step back. "You can do this!"

"One," I count off. I close my eyes.

"Two!" Lorrie cheers. Then, together, we cry, "Three!" and I jump in the air. My feet come down on the carpet, and I fling my eyes open—practically smelling the Olive Garden breadsticks and my mom's perfume—only to see that I'm still in Buck's trailer, with Lorrie standing before me, aghast.

Heat crawls up my neck and cheeks. I press my palms against my forehead. "Ugh—*I knew it*, I *knew* this wouldn't work! This is so stupid!"

Lorrie slaps both her hands over her eyes and shrieks. I jump, startled, and look at her.

"It's so easy!" she shouts. Her cheeks are burning red, her eyes screwed shut. I step back, eyes wide, as she begins to pace. Buck wraps his arm around my shoulder and kisses my forehead.

"It's okay, babe, you'll get it," he whispers as Lorrie continues to rant.

"It's so simple! Why can't you get it—you're me! You should know this!" she shouts. I clench my jaw and Buck holds me tighter.

"Hey, she's doing the best she can," Buck says. "Give her a break."

"No! No, we can't take breaks!" Lorrie shouts. "I'm a *child* and I can do it—why can't you? You think of a moment—literally any moment—and then you just close your eyes and—" Lorrie vanishes in a ball of electricity. Power flickers through the house, then returns to normal.

"Huh," Buck whispers. "Well, that's ironic."

I pinch the bridge of my nose and slump into the beanbag. This day couldn't get any worse if it tried. My throat aches and the tired seeps into my bones, sucking at the marrow, draining me of everything I am or was.

"Is...she coming back?" Buck asks, looking around the trailer.

I sigh and throw my hands in the air. "Who knows! It took her an *entire week* to come back last time."

Buck whirls around to face me. "A week? You've known about her for a week and haven't said anything?"

I huff and look up at him. "What did you want me to do, Buck? I thought I was going crazy!"

"Well," Buck shifts, "why *didn't* you tell me?"

I shake my head. "You wouldn't have believed me—heck, *I* didn't believe me…"

Now Buck looks like I've hit him. I feel a pang of guilt twist in my gut, followed quickly by a rush of heat. It fills my lungs like steam and I sit up, glaring at him.

"What?" I snap. "You wouldn't have! You would have thought I was going crazy, and you would have tried to get me to tell my dad so that we could talk or whatever, and it wouldn't have helped!"

Buck opens his mouth, but I'm too fired up to back down now.

"You wouldn't have helped! And now Lorrie's gone again, only to come back God knows *when*, with Miller out there knowing God knows *what,* and no matter what I do or try, I can't do *anything* to fix it!" I slump again into the beanbag and cover my face with my hands. "Lorrie's right," I whisper, "I should be able to do this…"

Silence falls in the trailer for a while, and Buck just stands there. Then I hear him walk over to me. He sits in the beanbag next to me and I peek at him through the cracks in my hands.

"I believed you today, didn't I?" His voice is barely above a whisper. My heart clenches, and I pull my legs into my lap. Buck's lips are pressed together, his hands clasped in front of him.

"Yeah," I finally whisper back.

"And you've tried for less than an hour, right?"

"...Yeah..."

Buck nods. "Yeah..."

In the quiet that follows, Buck reaches out and presses his big toe against my ankle. He closes his eyes, lets his head fall back, and gives a small sigh. Then he whispers, "I love you."

Pressure builds behind my eyes. I shift, then crawl over into the beanbag with him. I curl against his side and let my head rest against his collarbone, then I close my eyes.

"I love you, too."

Ten

I KEEP MY EYES CLOSED, my head resting against the window. I can feel the pane rattling against my forehead as Buck drives me home. It's long past dark now, the stars twinkling in the sky. Country music crackles from the radio. A simple, twangy song with a male singer. His voice is a low rumble as he sings about his wife leaving him.

It isn't long before we pull up to the front of my house. I crack open my eye and see that the lights are still on inside. I sit up. *Did Dad wait up for me?* Something I'm too tired to name stirs in my chest and I find myself drawn to the house.

Buck yawns aggressively behind me and rubs his forehead with his fingers.

"You okay?" I ask as I pick up my purse from the floor of the truck.

Buck nods. "Yeah, just...long day."

I chuckle. "Yeah…"

I should thank him for putting up with me. Thank him for all the ways he's stayed by me. I don't deserve his love.

Instead, I lean over and press a kiss against his temple, then I slip out of the truck.

"Love you!" he calls.

"Love you, too," I smile and let the truck slam shut. I jog up the porch and push on the door. It swings open. Dad left it unlocked *again.* I click my tongue and step inside.

"Dad—how many times do I have to tell you!" I bump the door closed with my hip. I throw my shoes against the wall, drop my purse on the wooden cabinet beside the door, and pad into the kitchen. "You can't leave the front door un…"

The kitchen is empty. A quick peek in the living room tells me no one's there either. I'm just about to check upstairs when the basement door bangs open. I yelp and jump behind the kitchen island. Dad stands at the top of the basement stairs, huffing. His face is red and his glasses are askew. His eyes are bloodshot and red-rimmed, as though he'd spent the entire day staring at a computer screen without blinking.

Of course he wasn't actually waiting up for me. I'm such an idiot.

"Dad," I groan and pinch the bridge of my nose. "What—"

"Lorrie!" he cries.

My stomach drops. *He knows. How does he know—how did he find out?*

"What?" I whisper.

He takes two quick steps toward me and grabs my hands. "Lorrie—I—" His face screws up and he shakes his head. "I-I mean, *Lorraine*, sorry. Lorraine! I did it—the Machine—the readings—you have to come see it!"

I can't find the will to protest as my dad drags me down the basement stairs and over to the large computer monitors on the other side of the Machine.

These computers run simulations, track different types of radiation in the Earth's atmosphere, and way more science-y mumbo jumbo that an artistic geek like me could ever understand.

My dad turns sideways and slips between the desk and the plastic shield, tugging on my arm to join him. I roll my eyes and shimmy into the tight space with him.

"What is it now?" I ask, arms crossed. I swallow tightly and look at the monitors—and can already feel a headache building as I try to understand what I'm staring at.

"There." My dad points at the top left screen. It's a graph of some sort, clearly tracking...*something.*

I squint and look closer. The line spikes on the chart every now and then. To artistic eyes like mine, they seem as useless as my math tutor was—well, all the lines except for two, which spike high above the others. I feel my stomach clench as I look at them. I clamp my hands down around my arms and go from crossing my arms to hugging myself.

"*It* worked," my dad whispers. The blue of the screen reflects off his smile. It casts his face in an eerie glow. The graph reflects in his glasses, consuming all he sees, all he is. I'm tempted to wave a hand in front of his face. Would he flinch? Would he even see me at all, next to this stupid freakin' machine?

"*What* am I *looking* at?" I snap.

"Oh—right, right. See—see this here—that's when we last tested the Machine. You see, when tachyons travel they leave energy in the air. Well—*leave* isn't really the right word. More like *displace*. Anyway, we can track that displaced energy—that's what the spikes on this chart are. Then, again, just this morning! Do you see it? Do you see what this means?"

I lean forward, pressing against the desk, staring at the spiky blue line.

"What does it mean?" My voice wavers. My throat is suddenly dry.

"Time travel is happening—*somewhere*, here, by the Machine. It could be little—like a fly, or-or a dust particle—but something changed. I-I opened a path or...or something! Which means we're close, Lorraine. We are so close to figuring this thing out!"

I swallow. If my dad has the tech in his basement to track Lorrie's time traveling...what does Miller, aka *Huson Labs*, know about it?

"That's..." terrifying? Horrible? A complete disaster? I shake my head and press my lips together. My legs are trembling as I quickly push myself out of the small, cramped space. "I—cool, Dad. Listen, I'm tired, so, I-I'm heading to bed. Don't stay up too much later, okay?"

My dad waves me off. "Pasta's on the stove!" he calls cheerily as he continues to stare at the monitors. Knowing him, he'll forget we even had this conversation, and he'll end up falling asleep, slumped over his monitors, his numbers, his theories.

I hurry up the stairs, through the living room, and into my bedroom. I barely let myself breathe until I'm safe inside with the door shut firmly behind me.

This is bad news. No—worse than bad news, *this is a disaster.*

I pace my room for an hour, racking my brain to try and come up with something—anything—I can do. But there's nothing. I'm not smart like my Dad. I can't time travel like Lorrie can. I have no way to contact her and warn her about this mess—about what this could mean.

"Ugh!" I cry and flop onto my bed. "This is hopeless!"

I drag my hands over my face and roll over to stare at the window. Sitting on the window seat is my laptop. Slowly, I push myself up onto my elbows... I don't have a way to contact Lorrie...or do I?

I look at my laptop, the thumb drive still stuck on the side. I scramble up from the bed, kicking off the blankets that tangle my leg, and rush to the laptop. I flip it open, heart pounding.

I click record and stare into the black, beady eye of the camera.

"Lorrie..." I feel silly as I speak but I push past it with a shake of my head. "I... Dad's picking up on your traveling from his computers, and if Dad knows, then his old work—Huson Labs—probably knows something is up, too. Dad'll be arrested if you keep carelessly zapping from the past to the present, so...be careful. It's..." I stop and look at the time. "It's nearly midnight here. July 24th, 2018... Come back so we can talk about the plan, and don't go anywhere else!"

I go to end the video and hesitate, my finger hovering over the mouse. I click my tongue and look back into the camera.

"And when you travel, make sure you treat it like a walk in the park, or whatever—don't touch anything, don't talk to anyone you shouldn't, and *be respectful*!"

I end the video and save it to the thumb drive. I sit, holding it in my hand, then move over to my bed. I'll have to send it through the Machine to actually get it to her, but my dad will want to test the Machine again soon enough. I just have to send it back with whatever we test. I look at the dresser, eying the dozens of cards from Miller and the small handheld taser I keep next to them. I shift, then sit back on the soft quilts, my shoulders tight. I stare into the darkness, and I wait.

Eleven

MY PHONE BUZZES. I crack open my eyes. Sunlight trickles through the slits in the window shutters on my left. I yawn and sit up. My back aches from the odd position I'd slept in. I rub my eyes. My phone buzzes again. I struggle to find it in the piles of blankets and pillows. When I finally find it, I glance at the screen.

11:37am, July 25th, 2018.

I yawn and swipe down to look at the notifications. My heart stops. Twenty-seven missed calls from Buck and ten texts. I scramble out of my nest of blankets and swipe my phone open.

Lorraine

answer your phone

Please it's an emergency

LORRAINE

WAKE UP

I can't believe this

mom and Papa are going to kill me

Lorraine, this is a real emergency.

My love, my light, my angel, if you don't answer your phone I am never going to make you mac & cheese again. That is a threat.

Lorraine please

I am running. I'm running.

LORRAINE THEY ARE IN MY TRAILER

I swipe to his contact and dial. Within the first ring, he answers. "Buck?" I ask. "Buck—what's going on."

"They were *here,* Lorraine!" Buck hisses into the phone. He sounds out of breath. Between each word, he sucks in air.

I scramble off the bed and hold my phone to my ear with both hands. "Who? Who was there?"

"Huson Laboratory!" Buck cries. "They were knocking on my door. That stupid Miller—had a—*warrant*! Papa's—going to—kill me!"

"A warrant?!" I yelp. "How can he have a warrant—he's not a cop! Buck, where are you?" I race to my dresser and grab a clean shirt. I throw it on, then struggle into an old pair of jeans I'd scooped off the floor.

"In—the corn—fields!" Buck cries. "I didn't know what to do, so—so I ran! They're going through my trailer!"

"Okay—okay, Buck, calm down. Are they chasing you still?"

"No—I don't think so—I don't think they saw me leave—I just—ran!"

I grab my house keys off the dresser and struggle to tug on a tennis shoe. "Okay—Buck, I'm coming. Just—just—stay in the cornfields!"

"Lorraine—Lorraine, you don't understand. Miller—he knows!"

I stop with my shoe half on. "Knows what?"

"He knows about Lorrie—I heard him through the door—I don't know how, but he's tracking her!"

"Okay," I shake my head, "we'll figure it out—just stay hidden. I'm coming to get you!" I tug the shoe on and rush out the bedroom door. One emergency at a time. First things first, I have to convince my dad to let me borrow his car—which would be a lot easier if I actually had my license.

I try not to curse at myself as I rush down the stairs and fly into the kitchen. Dad's at the stove, boiling water. He looks up and smiles.

"Hey, sleepyhead," he motions to the water, "I'm making some tea! Do you—"

"Buck's in trouble. I need your car." The words rush out before I can stop them. My dad's shoulders drop, his mouth parting, and his eyes widen. Then he turns off the stove and stalks past me, out of the kitchen. I blink. "Dad? Didn't you hear? Buck's in—"

"Trouble," my dad finishes. He grabs his coat off the peg on the wall and fishes his keys out of the pocket. He turns to me, slings the jacket over his shoulder, and nods toward the front door. "Let's go."

My stomach clenches. He can't come—he'd ask questions— and if he asked questions, he'd learn about Lorrie.

"Dad, no! I need to—"

"Family is the most important thing, Lorraine. I know you don't like it when I talk about marriage and…well…all that, but Buck's family. We don't leave him behind."

I think about all the times I've waited for Buck outside of work. All the times my dad could have come to get me instead. I shake my head. Heat begins to rise in my neck and shoulders.

"Dad! Buck is—I can't—" I press my palms against my forehead. "He doesn't want you to see him like this, so can you *please* just give me the keys to your car?"

My dad hesitates, his hand resting on the silver doorknob. He swallows, glancing at me, then looks behind him at the door. "What sort of trouble is he in?"

"It's... He's..." My tongue feels swollen in my mouth. I lick my lips and shove my hands in my pockets. *Buck is going to kill me for this.* "He's real embarrassed by it, so...I'm...not sure he wants me to share it with you..."

My dad frowns. He looks down at the car keys in his hand. "But...but you hate driving."

Oh, sure, what a fine time for him to know something about me! I shake off the irritation with a shrug and lean against the wall.

"Buck's been showing me how to drive," I whisper. "I'm fine on the back roads." Another lie. Buck's been begging to teach me to drive for over a year now, and each time I've resolutely refused. I don't need another thing on my plate right now.

My dad seems like he's caught between two strings, each one pulling him in a different direction. Finally, he runs his hand over his stubbled jaw and glances into the family room. I can tell his eyes fall on the mantel where the picture of my mom is, because his shoulders drop and he quickly looks to the floor.

"Well..." My dad shifts and tosses me the keys. I catch them, my mouth dropping. *That worked?!* My dad clears his throat.

"Just…drive safe, okay? And-and call me if you need anything, anything at all! Family is—"

"The most important thing!" I yell as I book it out the front door. "Got it! Thanks!"

I race to the red minivan, rapidly clicking the unlock button. I throw open the door and slip into the driver's side. My heart is beating like a wild gorilla against my chest. I run my palms over my jeans and swallow, looking in the rearview mirror. Family is the most important thing, and my mom is out there, waiting for me to save her.

I'll have to face far greater things than driving to accomplish that. I tell this to myself over, and over, and over again as I turn the car on. The engine rumbles and the lights on the dashboard flash. It needs an oil change, and the check engine light is a permanent feature on this vehicle. I shut my eyes. Suck in a shaky breath. With a trembling hand I shift the car into reverse—I then slam on the breaks to keep from rolling backwards down the driveway.

"Okay," I whisper to myself. I ease off the pedal and look into the mirror. "Okay… You can do this."

How hard can driving really be?

Twelve

REALLY HARD! Driving is really freakin' hard and it's why I don't ever want to actually get my license—it's stupid and the human race wasn't meant to travel over thirty miles an hour, let alone sixty, while strapped into a metal death trap!

Each tap of the brakes sends me reeling forward. Each time a car whizzes past me, I flinch. I can feel the car move with each gust of wind, bounce with each bump in the road. Something inside keeps beeping at me, and it takes me fifteen minutes to realize my door was never properly shut. There's a lot to focus on, okay?

I pull off the highway onto a back-road, the tires crunching over the gravel as I approach a creek. It's a small thing, winding and twisting along the edge of the west side of the cornfields. It lets out by one of the gates, a perfect back entrance to Buck's family's property. I push the brakes and everything in the car shifts forward as the vehicle stops. I take a breath and, with a shaking hand, shift the car into park. I sit for a second in the silence, the car still rumbling. I rest my forehead on the steering wheel and suck in a breath. That was *awful.*

I pull out my phone and text Buck to meet me at the third gate, on the west side of the property. It's far enough away from the main entrance without being so far out of the way that I can't drive there.

I let out a breath, shut my eyes, and lean against the headrest. Only five minutes on the highway, but those five minutes were enough to last me a lifetime. The one thing I've learned from this ordeal? I am never going to drive again.

It takes him fifteen minutes to get to me. With every minute that passes, I find myself caught between staring at the dashboard clock and at the highway behind me. Cars fly by, and each time I spot a streak of silver I hold my breath—only to let it out when the car inevitably drives by.

A knock raps on the passenger side window, and I jolt. It's Buck. I quickly slip out of the car and run to him, wrapping my arms around him.

He's struggling to breathe, his face red and flushed. Sweat drips down his forehead as he holds me tight, burying his head into my neck.

"Thank you," he rasps out. "I didn't... Thank you."

"Here." I pass him the keys and then slip into the passenger's side.

Buck looks at the keys, then up at me, eyes wide. "Where are we going?"

"My place," I say.

He gets into the driver's seat. He opens his mouth to say something but stops, eying the rearview mirror. "Get down!" he hisses, sliding down in his seat. I spin around, staring out the back window.

Two police cruisers have pulled off the highway. My heart lurches into my throat. Do they know? Did Miller get the police involved already? I hunch down in my seat, holding my breath. I can hear their tires rumble over the dirt—can practically feel them zeroing in on the red sedan, on Buck and me hiding inside.

Did they find out about Lorrie? How? What will we say if they see us in my dad's car? I press my forehead against the armrest. I gulp down a breath—and another. It's not enough.

Would they know I drove? What happens when you drive without a license—does this car have insurance? Is it even registered? What happens when you're pulled over without insurance or registration?

And if Miller already has the police involved, what does that mean for Dad? Would he be arrested—would I be all alone?

"They're gone." Buck puts a hand on my shoulder. I look up. Sure enough, the two police cruisers are speeding off down the dirt road to who knows where. They haven't even slowed down.

I let out a breath and close my eyes. "We're out of time," I whisper.

"What?" Buck asks. I look at him.

"We are out of time," I repeat. "I have to remember how to time travel. Now."

Thirteen

I HAVE BUCK PARK DOWN THE STREET from the house. Together, we sneak down the street and into my backyard. I crouch low as we creep along the side of the house. I pick at the peeling paint. It flakes off without much effort. I flick the particles off my fingers as we sneak past the kitchen windows, keeping low. We come to the side door right next to the kitchen. I pull down on the handle, gently easing the door open a crack, and listen for my dad.

Every Tuesday and Thursday, around the time the sun begins to set, my dad leaves the house to walk around the neighborhood. He says that it's "good for his soul" and always asks me to join him. But I can't stand the mosquitoes in the summer, or the moths in the fall, or the nip of the cold in the winter, and my allergies always act up in the spring, so I've never gotten around to joining him.

But, for once, him being gone will be the perfect opportunity to do what needs to be done. Buck and I wait, keeping the door cracked, as I listen for my dad. I can hear him whistling, bustling about the kitchen. I stay quiet until I hear the front door open and close. Then the house is quiet. My dad is gone. I let out a breath and step into the kitchen.

"Hurry up," I tell Buck as we head to the basement. "We don't have a lot of time."

"First things first," Buck asks, "why haven't we told your dad about Lorrie yet?"

We round the corner and come to the basement. I jiggle the handle. *Locked.* I click my tongue and step back. *Figures he remembers to lock this door...after all, it's protecting the one thing he actually cares about.* But he *has* to have a spare key around here somewhere.

"Check the junk drawers," I tell Buck as I walk back into the kitchen. I throw open the cabinets, searching for the gold key. Buck clears his throat. I turn to look at him. He's standing behind me, arms crossed, a single eyebrow raised.

I roll my eyes and turn back to searching the drawers. "*Because* Lorrie said that would ruin things." I shut the cabinets and move to the drawers.

Behind me, Buck starts searching the pantry. "Right," he

mutters, "and a thirteen-year-old knows exactly what to do with big, life-altering choices like that."

I roll my eyes again. "Twelve," I correct. "Besides, out of everyone involved in this situation, she's the only one who actually knows about time travel—being as she's the only one who's actually *done* it. If she says that telling my dad would ruin things, then I have to believe her."

"Lorraine, you promised that you'd tell him," Buck says. I stop and shut a drawer with my hip. I turn around, my arms tucked behind my back. He's standing across the kitchen, leaning against the counter.

"I will," I stress my words. "I promise. Just... I want to get a handle on this situation first. You *said* you'd let me figure this out."

Buck frowns and we fall silent for a moment. Then he pulls his hand out of his pockets and holds up the gold key. I grin. Together, we hurry to the basement, unlock the door, and rush down the stairs.

The Machine looms in the middle of the room. The wires sprawl across the ground like a spilled bowl of spaghetti. Buck sucks in a breath next to me as we stare at it.

My head spins. Being down here without Dad's insistent and endless chatter is...weird.

"Right, let's get this thing on," I say, picking my way across the wires and tubes. "Buck, can you start it up from the computers? I think I need to plug in some of those cords over there." I stop when Buck doesn't follow me. He stays where he is on the cold, concrete floor.

"I... Babe, I'm not sure about this," he whispers. I stare at him silently until he shifts, sighs, and follows me to the computers. He slides behind the shield. His fingers hesitate over the keyboard. "What exactly is your plan here?"

I kick at a tube on the ground, pushing it closer to the Machine. This place is a wreck. "I need to remember how to time travel, and everything else we've tried hasn't exactly worked."

"You tried, like, twice," Buck protests.

"And it didn't work!" I huff a strand of my hair out of my face. "We're just going to start it up so I can jog my memory. We're not trying to make it *do* anything. How hard can it be?"

Buck shrugs, and I slip out from behind the shield. I've been forced to watch so many of my dad's failed test experiments over the years, it isn't exactly hard to figure out what needs to be plugged in where. At least, I hope it's all in the right place. If not, what's the worst that could happen? *Another* failed experiment?

Finally, after I have everything plugged in, I rejoin Buck behind the plastic shield at the computers.

I hug myself as I stare at the screens. "Please tell me you know what you're looking at."

"Your dad has the coolest setup," he whispers. Then, he points at the top left monitor. "That's interesting—must be what Miller is picking up on his signals—look. That's weird…it says we're in a spike right now."

I peer around him. "What?"

Buck shifts out of the way. Sure enough, the lines are moving into an upward tick of tachyon radiation—or whatever it is. I look around the room. It's normal. Well, as normal as a basement full of illegal scientific equipment can be.

"Turn it on." I step away from the computer and stare at the Machine. I hug myself a little tighter. My stomach churns. *I hate this room.* Buck's fingers fly over the keyboard. The lights above flick off. The arms of the Machine begin to spin, slow at first then faster and faster.

I want to close my eyes, but this time I refuse. Instead, I keep staring at the Machine. A wave of heat bursts from the center—I can feel it even with the protective shield in front of us. A wind picks up around us, tousling the papers, clawing at my hair.

An intense dread comes upon my chest, the one I always feel when Dad tests the Machine. I grit my teeth and press my nose against the plastic shield. Keep watching—I have to keep watching.

Then, in the back of my mind, I feel something. A memory that's long since faded. I suck in a breath. It's like it's on the tip of my tongue. Like it's trapped just behind a glass wall. I put my hand on the shield. I refuse to so much as blink. I won't miss this—not this time.

"C'mon," I whisper. "Remember."

And just when the memory tickles the surface of my brain's calm waters, it dives back down—deep down—and vanishes into the depths. The moment it does, the lights around me flicker, splutter, and then explode one by one. I shriek and stumble back. Sparks rain from the ceiling. I look at the monitors—the top left one has numbers rushing up until they're off the chart. My stomach sinks. *This isn't good.* The tubes along the floor wriggle and writhe like worms. The Machine's spinning lurches to a grinding stop—something stuck in the gears—did we not plug something in right? Did the arms catch on a tube? A plume of black smoke coughs up from the platform in the center of the Machine. It shifts, bubbling up like tar.

A zap echoes around the room—a bright, hot light flashes to my left. Lorrie drops from the blue ball of light and sits up. She takes one look around the room, then to me, her mouth drawn open like a fish out of water.

"What are you doing?" she shrieks. "Are you—"

The power pulses. Electricity surges through the wires, the pumps, the lights in the ceiling. They crackle and then burst, tiny red sparks spraying. A wave of heat shoots out from the Machine. I cough and wave my hand in front of my face, trying to clear the smoke. I look back at the Machine—my heart stops—a fire has burst to life at the center.

"Shut it off!" I shout.

"I'm trying—I'm trying!" Buck cries as I dash out from behind the safety shield. I rush to the stairs and haul the red fire extinguisher off the wall. I turn toward the Machine. Orange flames dance next to the glowing blue pipes. The metal's charring, tinting black. The heat beats against my face. I wince, raising the fire extinguisher.

"No! No, you'll ruin it! We can still get it to work!" Lorrie steps in front of me. I shove her aside, aim the fire extinguisher, and let it blast. White foam shoots from the nozzle and douses everything—the Machine, the flames, the wires, the tubes.

I keep at it until the orange flames aren't reaching their molten hands out toward me. I hold the trigger until the heat fades, until I'm left in complete and utter darkness. I stand there, gasping for breath—coughing when I inhale the smoke—until Buck's hand is wrapping around my own and he's gently pulling the fire extinguisher from my grasp. I hear it clunk against the concrete floor.

"Where are the stairs?" Buck asks.

I cough and rub my eyes—they burn. They *sting*. "F-follow me." I hold his hand and together we feel our way out of the basement and to the stairs. We struggle until we come to the door, then burst into the family room. Lorrie is standing in the center, staring at the mantel where Mom's urn is. She's looking at the framed pictures, all of Mom.

I suck down a clear breath and look at Buck, then back to Lorrie. Tears streak down her round cheeks. "Lorrie?" I ask.

"You didn't remember," she accuses. She swipes away the tears with her palms. "You didn't remember, and now the Machine is broken, and we'll *never* save Mom."

Fourteen

I RUSH TOWARD LORRIE and wrap her in my arms before I can stop myself. I hug her tight against my chest, then bend down to her eye level. "Don't say that. We can fix this. We just... I can fix it. Together, we'll fix it!"

"No! No, we can't and it's all your—" Lorrie snaps her mouth closed. Someone's whistling. Both of us scramble toward the window in the family room to stare out at the porch. Dad is walking up the steps to the front door. I look down at Lorrie as she looks up to me, face pale.

"I... We need the help," I whisper. "Maybe Dad can—"

"No!" she hisses. She clenches her trembling hands at her side. I can hear the keys jangling, clacking against the front door.

"We need someone who knows what they're doing," Buck says.

Lorrie whirls around toward him. "I *know* what I'm *doing*— and *he* will *ruin everything*!"

The front door opens. The hairs on the back of my neck rise.

"Lorraine? You home yet, sweetie?" Dad calls out.

Lorrie scowls. "Don't," she whispers, then vanishes in a flash of electricity.

The power flickers through the house for a moment, then shuts off again. I freeze. I can hear my dad pad through the hallway into the kitchen.

Buck comes up behind me and puts a hand on my shoulder. "Family is everything, right?" he whispers. I nod.

"What happened to the power?" my dad calls from the kitchen. "Lorraine? Are you home?"

Buck presses a kiss against my temple. "Maybe the first step to fixing your family is fixing your relationship with your dad?"

I stand still, my mind racing. If I tell Dad about Lorrie, there's no saying what will happen. He would say that, when traveling through time, you should treat your surroundings like you treat nature on a hike: Don't take anything, don't break anything, and make sure nobody knows you've been there. The past shouldn't be changed, he'll say. We can't play God. Bad things happen when we play God.

But if I did nothing…would we be able to save Mom?

I look to the basement stairwell. Even in the dark, I can see the smoke that's made its way up the stairs. It's billowing into the house. Dad comes into the family room and stops.

"Lorraine?" he asks. "Why are you in the dark, silly?"

Buck clears his throat and pats my shoulder. "I'm...gonna go grab your dad's car," he mutters. "Good luck."

"You're leaving me to deal with this on my own?" I snap.

Buck smiles. "No, no, I'll be back, but...yeah. Good luck."

I watch as Buck turns, awkwardly nods at my dad, and then shuffles out of the house. I clear my throat and try desperately not to think about my dad's life's work, which is currently smoldering far beneath our feet.

"Lorraine, are you okay?" my dad asks, his voice quiet. I sigh and, even though it's dark and I can't really see him anyway, I drop my gaze to the ground.

"Hey, Dad? We...we need to talk."

Fifteen

MY LEG BOUNCES UP AND DOWN as I sit on the worn yellow couch in our living room. My dad is across from me on the brown leather sofa. We've slid open the windows behind him to try and clear out most of the smoke. Between us are a bunch of candles on the wooden coffee table. We'd set them up quickly, just until we could get the power to come back on. Subtly, I glance to my right, at the gray mantel, and meet my mother's eyes... Would she be upset with me if it were her in Dad's place? I shake my head and look back at my dad. His hands are folded in his lap, his eyes staring straight ahead, his lips pressed firmly together. He's waiting for *me* to talk, for once. The one time he's silent and is waiting for me to talk, it's because I destroyed something. *Great.*

I press my palms together and stare at the flickering flame of the candle and say, "I want to start by saying I understand if you can't forgive me."

My dad smooths his palms on his khaki pants. "Lorraine, what happened? Let's just...let's start from there."

I nod, swallow hard, and stare down at my tennis shoes. How do you tell your father that you've destroyed his lifelong passion?

I grit my teeth together. Better to rip off the Band-Aid and just come out with it. "Dad, I destroyed your TIME Machine." I close my eyes. I can hear his sharp intake of breath. I continue. "I went down there when I wasn't supposed to, and messed around with it like an idiot, and the Machine...caught fire. I-I'm fine and so is Buck and Lor—well..."

I clear my throat and open my eyes. My dad is sagging against the back of the couch, his hand pressed against his forehead. I press my palms together and suck in a breath.

"I'm... I'll fix it, or—I mean, I'll help fix it, I just... The tests you were doing..." My tongue feels swollen, and my stomach is trying to break the world record of how many twists it can do. Before I can stop myself, the lies of appeasement tumble from my lips. "I just—I was so interested and curious and I let that get the better of me. I'm sorry!"

My dad lets his arm drop to his side. He stares up at the ceiling, his eyes dancing back and forth. He purses his lips, then rubs his hand over his jaw.

"Dad?" I whisper. He stays still, and I look at the front door, praying that Buck will walk in and save me like he always does. But he doesn't. The door stays closed and I'm left to sit in the awkward, thick silence.

I let my head hang low and run a hand through my hair.

"Lorraine," my dad finally speaks, "I'm..." His voice sounds like a worn piece of paper. He clears his throat and looks at me. "I'm glad you told me. Let's...let's go see the damage. I'm sure we can fix it."

My eyes widen as my dad stands up and heads to the basement. "Dad? You don't understand. The entire thing was *on fire*. I used the fire extinguisher and everything, it was—"

"Fixable, I'm sure of it." My dad turns to me. "Lorraine, I forgive you. Next time, if you're going to destroy the Machine, let's do it together, huh?" He laughs at his own joke and I stare, slack-jawed, as he grabs a candle and heads down into the basement.

This doesn't make any sense—he should be furious with me. But there isn't any anger or shouting. There's just that infuriatingly quiet...*forgiveness*. Bile rises in the back of my throat and I look back at the yellow couch. I feel nauseous.

"Lorraine, aren't you coming?" Dad hollers from downstairs and I'm jolted from my thoughts. I'll think about this later. I stand, grab my own candle, and walk down the stairs.

I join him in the basement, and together we stare at the contorted bits of melted metal and plastic tubes. Blue, shimmery liquid has seeped into the ground from where the tubes had burst free from the Machine, and in the dim candlelight it looks more like a grotesque monster than a time machine.

"I told you. It's bad," I whisper.

My dad puts his arm around my shoulder and squeezes. "Wouldn't be the first time it's looked like this, and it certainly won't be the last," he smiles. He looks down at me, and his eyes get all misty. "I'm just glad you finally understand how interesting this is! Time travel—exciting stuff, isn't it?"

I quickly look away. He gives my shoulder one final squeeze, then says, "Let's call Buck back in. I'm sure we can figure this out in no time!"

Sixteen

BUCK AND I SIT AROUND the dining room table, a single candle between us. The tiny flame dances and flares in the darkness around
it, as if it doesn't care that it's the only thing providing light.

My dad had gone outside to the breaker box to figure out
how to get the power back on. Luckily, it seems like it's just our
house that's lost electricity. An angry call from the neighbors is
delayed—for now.

"Doesn't it make you wonder?" Buck whispers.

"About what?" I ask.

Buck rubs his thumb over my knuckles. The candlelight flickers in his breath. "About forgiveness?"

I move back and cross my arms. My eyebrows pinch together.
"Not really."

Buck frowns and reaches across the table again. He grabs my
hand and pulls me forward. He presses a kiss to my knuckles.

"Okay, Lorraine... Have you heard from Lorrie yet?"

"No," I whisper. "I haven't. I don't know why... Maybe she's mad at me—maybe she's *never* coming back."

"Now, why on earth would she be mad at you?" Buck asks. I roll my eyes. He leans forward, wiggling his brow. "Does *that* make you wonder about forgiveness?"

"Buck," I warn.

He throws both hands in the air in mock-surrender and shrugs. "Okay, alright, sorry! I'll stop!"

He laughs, and a smile tugs at my lips. I press them together and stare at the single flickering candle flame.

What if Lorrie never comes back? What if we never get the Machine working again? What if this is all pointless?

Despite what I've told Buck, I *am* wondering about forgiveness. How can my father move so easily past the complete and total destruction of his life's work? An uncomfortable pit has formed in the center of my stomach, and no matter which way I wriggle or squirm, it stays put, refusing to move. If it had been a different project—a different machine, something he didn't care about as much...

Suddenly, the lights flicker on around us. I sigh, lean forward, and blow out the single dancing flame. It extinguishes in half a millisecond. The only evidence of its life is the light-gray smoke that drifts up from the wick, dispersing in the air. I stand and grab the candlestick.

"C'mon, let's get these cleaned up," I tell Buck.

Together, we collect the candles spread around the dining and living room. Just as we finish up, my dad barrels inside. He skids around the corner from the kitchen and makes a mad dash toward the basement.

"Dad?" I call—and then I'm following him, rushing down the stairs. I cough as we descend into the basement. The smoke lingers in the air like a midnight fog. I wave my hand through the air and watch as the gray smoke curls and shifts at my touch.

My dad shoves over the protective shield in his haste and stands at his computer, his fingers dancing across the keyboard.

"What are we looking at?" Buck appears from behind me. Together, we walk over to my dad and peer at the screen.

"There was something different about the last test—before the Machine caught," he said. "It's never done that before—the spontaneous flames, that is. Each test is recorded and immediately logged into this system so I can compare them. See—oh, look! Look! The radiation in the room spikes here, but...no, this doesn't make sense..."

My stomach clenches. "What?"

"Look—" my dad tilts the monitor toward us. "The radiation

in the room spikes here, but...that's before the test even started... How strange!"

Buck and I share a glance.

My father tugs the monitor back toward him. Despite my dislike of the sciences, I find myself stepping behind him, trying to take a look at the screens. I catch a glimpse of the spikes on the chart.

"This here—that's when the test starts. The radiation is significantly higher than with other tests..." He looks back at me. "What did you do differently?"

I think back to Lorrie—how she appeared right as the Machine had started to malfunction. I shrug. "I don't know. I... just...started the Machine up."

Buck clears his throat and nudges me.

"What's the plan for fixing the Machine?" I ask and clap my hands together. My dad grins, then darts away from the computers toward the Machine. Buck shakes his head but says nothing. I let out a breath of relief, then step over the plastic shield and watch as my dad darts around the molten metal catastrophe before us. He's already knee-deep in the disaster I've created, soot coating his pant legs.

"In theory, I have"—Dad grunts as he lifts one of the metal arms—"all the parts I need to weld, I keep extra on hand. The only problem"—another grunt as he threw the arm to the side—"is the tachyon particles."

My nose scrunches. "The what?"

"Tachyon particles. That's how the Machine runs. But to be able to harness the tachyons, we had to slow them down, thus the blue liquid—for the Machine. You see, photons slow down in the liquid. Not by much, but enough for us to be able to—"

"Okay," I interrupt. "We don't need all the science behind this. How do we get the Tocky-ons?"

"*Tachy*ons," Dad corrects. "That's just it. The equipment is at Huson Laboratory."

My shoulders drop and I groan. "Great, just *great*."

"What's the problem?" Buck asks. "Can't you just go pick some up?"

My dad and I whirl around to stare at him—and as we do, Dad trips on a wire and crash-lands in a pile of rubble. A poof of smoke and dust explodes from around him and he coughs, waving a hand in front of his face.

Buck stares dumbly at the two of us. "What?"

"Huson Laboratory for Research and Development is a privately funded research facility." My dad struggles to his feet. He kicks off a stray wire and runs a hand over his face, leaving a smear of soot across his forehead. For a second, I'm glad he never leaves the house. I can't imagine he'd bother fixing his appearance to do so.

My dad continues, "Our goal was to discover things most scientists would dismiss as impossible—and then to make that impossible a reality!"

"Oh, you mean like time travel," Buck says.

My dad grins. "Exactly! Time travel, shrink rays, death rays, mind control—you name it, we'd dream it. If it were in a fictional world, Mrs. Huson wanted it in real life."

I dust off a smear of soot on my jeans. "It's beyond me how that woman ever got funded in the first place."

"Well," my dad shrugs and turns back to the Machine. "You invent a shrink ray or two, and suddenly all sorts of people want dibs on your stuff. Billionaires, countries—our top client is the United States Department of Defense. All very top secret and hush-hush."

I stop and look up. "The *what*?"

Buck's eyes widen. "Wait—you created time travel for the US Government?!"

My dad shakes his head. "No, I *was* creating time travel for the US Government. Not anymore. Why'd you think we're in the basement instead of a top secret research facility right now?" My dad snorts at his own joke and throws another charred bit of metal to the side. I wince as it clatters against the ground.

You'd think that, in all of my dad's ramblings and lectures, at *some* point he would've care to mention that he was investigated by *the United States Department of Defense.* I pinch the bridge of my nose and suck in a quick breath. *What a nightmare.* If Dad is a potential security leak to top secret, *classified* inventions that the *US Government* has called dibs on, no wonder Huson Lab has been such a pain in the butt about the accident.

A sudden thought chills me to my bones.

If Miller doesn't work for Huson Labs, but is interested in keeping my dad's time travel secret...who does *he work for?*

"Regardless," my dad continues, "I can't just 'pick up' the tachyons. I was fired, then blacklisted and forced to sign a stupid amount of paperwork—"

"An *NDA,* Dad!" I pull at a strand of my hair.

My dad keeps talking, as if he doesn't hear me. "If I ever tried to go back there, I'd probably be arrested on sight."

I narrow my eyes. "Then why are you smiling?"

"Because *I* know someone who *does* have access." My dad struggles his way out of the massacre that is his life's work and pulls out his flip phone. I watch as he puts the phone to his ear. It rings once...then twice...

My dad looks at me and a grin breaks out on his face. "Hey, Sebastian! How's your day going?"

Seventeen

BUCK AND I WALK OUT THE DOOR the next morning, my dad's keys in my hand. I grab Buck's hand and playfully push him with my hip. He glances down, raises a single brown eyebrow, then hip-bumps me back. I fly off the path and stumble into the grass on my right. Buck throws his head back and laughs.

"Buck, you're—" I cut myself off as I spot the silver sedan that's parked at the end of the driveway, blocking Dad's car. My heart climbs into my throat as I watch Miller step out of the vehicle. I slap Buck's arm and halt as Miller begins to walk up the driveway. "Buck!" I whisper.

Buck squares his shoulders, then, in a loud, deep voice, asks, "Can we help you?"

"Oh, I'm certain of it." Miller walks up the driveway until he's standing in front of us. I hold Buck's arm and squeeze. The corner of Miller's lip twitches up.

"Miller, would you mind moving your car?" I ask, and internally curse at how my voice shakes. I'm too nervous for this. What does he know? I swallow hard. "B-Buck and I are about to go out...on a date."

"Hmm..." Miller makes a show of scanning up and down the street. "Without Buck's vehicle?"

I frown. "Dad's letting us borrow the van for the weekend."

Miller smiles. I doubt it's because he's happy to see us. "Miss Sullivan, where were you last night?"

My heart is beating wildly against my chest, like a jackhammer against concrete. I feel Buck slip his hand into mine. I squeeze his hand.

"I...was home all night." I stare into the cold black lenses of Miller's glasses and see my pale, terrified expression staring back.

"Did you leave at all? Perhaps to pick up your boyfriend?"

"Why are you bothering us?" I snap. Wait—am I coming on too strong now? Was I too weak before? *What does Miller know?*

Buck wraps his arm around my shoulder.

"Listen, Miller, we've done nothing illegal," Buck says, and his warm voice is a drink of ice water on a hot summer day. It sets my nerves at ease. I let out a breath and let my eyes flutter shut as he continues. "So, if you don't mind, we'll be on our way—"

"We have a source that tells us there were high levels of radiation emitted in the area last night. The same sort of levels noted during the last failed experiment of the Machine that your father was employed to work on at Huson Laboratories." Miller takes another step toward us. I find a particular interest in his shiny black shoes. Like a spider hovering over a fly, I can feel him lean forward. His eyes bore into my skull like a drill into a cavity. Finally, I looked up until my eyes met his. He grins a wolfish sort of smile. "You wouldn't happen to know anything about that, would you, Lorraine?"

This is a disaster.

"Radiation?" I ask, blinking. I see Buck wince out of the corner of my eye. I press on. "I don't know much about radiation, other than it's bad for you. Oh, and apparently in our microwaves."

"Really." Miller doesn't seem impressed. I nod.

"Really," I mimic his voice. Then, I squeeze Buck's hand and stick my nose in the air. "Now, should I call the police and complain about your harassment, or will you let us go?"

"Lorraine Sullivan, I don't need to remind you that you and I are on turbulent grounds. I'm asking not as a friend—"

"Since when have we been friends?"

"—but as a military employee of the Department of Defense."

The breath is squeezed from my lungs. Around me, the world spins, and I hold onto Buck's hand to keep myself steady. There it is. The thing I've been fearing. He *isn't* just a nuisance—he's a government nuisance. He's a nuisance that can land our butts in jail.

"If you lie to me, well...what's to stop me from questioning if your father has kept his NDA? What's to stop me from pulling in the local authorities or the FBI? If things go the way they currently are, we're not talking about another slap on the wrist for your father." Miller speaks softly, yet each word sends a shiver down my spine.

I swallow and look up at Buck. To his credit, he stands still, his shoulders straight. He's brave in the face of condemnation. He's better than me.

I shake my head and look back at Miller. "Miller, you've visited me almost every Thursday for the past three years. You always demand an answer to the same freakin' question, and my answer is the same freakin' answer every single time," I say. "I haven't heard anything about my father's experiments, and if I did, I would call you." Then, in a mutter, I add, "I have a bazillion of your business cards, after all..."

Miller straightens, staring down at us, his jaw clenched. He blows a breath of air out through his nose, like a bull huffing, pawing at the ground, ready to charge at the red cloth.

"I'll be in touch—and remember, Lorraine...if this gets messy,

I did try to help you," he says. He turns, pulls at the cuffs of his suit, then stalks back to his silver sedan.

"What a jerk," Buck scoffs.

I watch as Miller slips inside his vehicle. I watch it pull away from the curb, drive down the street, and *finally* vanish around the corner. I suck in a breath and sag against Buck.

"We should go to the police." Buck clenches his teeth together. "He can't keep harassing you like this."

"No! We can't," I whisper and shut my eyes. "Buck, *he works for the government.* A-and if he knows something and we go to the police, what's to stop him from getting my dad arrested! Can you even serve jail time for that? Or-or will we just be fined? We can't afford a fine, let alone a good lawyer!"

"Hey, hey..." Buck runs his hand over the top of my head, smoothing fuzzy strands down. "It's gonna be fine. We haven't done anything illegal, so we're fine."

I stand up and look at him. "Buck, we *ran* the *Machine*!"

"That your *father* is banned from working on..." Buck shifts and looks up at the sky, then back down at me. "They never banned you. Or me, for that matter. We didn't sign any NDAs. We're just civilians. If anything, Huson Laboratory is the one that's in trouble."

"What do you mean?"

"Well, if Huson Labs had top secret government contracts, and then one of their employees breaks that agreement, it can't look good for them." Buck squeezes my hand, then tugs me toward the driveway. "If I were Huson Labs, I'd be more worried about losing business than some ex-scientist."

I blink once, then twice. He's right—granted, on a *technicality*—but he's right. I haven't done anything illegal…but as we clamber into the van and peel out of the driveway, I have a horrible, sinking suspicion that fact will soon be changing.

Eighteen

I LEAN BACK IN THE FRONT OF THE VAN, my legs brought tight to my chest, my head pressed uncomfortably against the window. We can't get the radio on, and my dad doesn't have an aux cord. All we have is my dad's old Spanish opera CDs. So, Spanish opera it is.

As we speed down the highway, I shift in my seat and look behind us. I stare at each silver sedan we pass—flinch as a patrol car zooms the opposite way down the highway. Like a spider tickling the back of my neck, I can't shake that nervous feeling that something isn't right. That something is watching us.

"So, when were you going to tell me you had an uncle?" Buck asks.

"'Cause he's not my uncle." I shrug. "He was my dad's college roommate, best man at the wedding, and favorite coworker."

Buck's nose scrunches. "I mean, I know your dad's always

talking to him, but how come he's never been over to the house?"

I shrug again. "Beats me if I know."

I'd never asked. If my dad wasn't going to ask about my friends, *or lack thereof*, I wasn't about to ask about his.

We come around a bend in the road and Buck taps on the brakes. Looming in front of us, in all its black glass glory, is a building. It's trespassing on the side of a mountain, with a nasty chain-link fence in front of it. Barbed wire circles the top of the fence, daring us to come forward. The building itself stands three stories tall. We pass a sign with brightly lit letters, saying, "Welcome to Huson Laboratory for Research and Development."

"Are we ready for this?" Buck asks, his knuckles white on the steering wheel.

I stare slack-jawed at the facility looming before us. The lab seems less like an office space and more like a military compound. It had been easier to say yes to my dad's request—to go and ask Sebastian for the tachyons in person—when I'd thought it was just an office.

"Ready as we'll ever be," I whisper. I pull out my phone and call Uncle Sebastian. My mouth is dry. I can't *believe* my dad thought this was a good idea. But, without Lorrie... *Do I really have any other choice?*

"Hey, Lorrie!" Sebastian's voice blares through the speaker and I jolt.

"Uh, actually, it's just Lorraine now," I say. *That nickname is going to be the death of me one day.*

"Oh, that's right! Sorry. Your dad mentioned that. Anyway, I've cleared you and Buck for a tour, so just drive up to the gate, give them your full name, and they should let you in. I'm in Building C—I'm coming up now to meet you out front."

Sebastian doesn't wait for me to answer. Instead, the phone goes quiet. I frown, looking down at it.

"Did he just hang up on you?" Buck asks.

"Oh, my gosh, this can't be happening," I whisper. I wasn't prepared for a security gate—*what if they don't let us in? What then? Worse, what if Miller knows we're coming here? What if—*

"What did he say?" Buck asks. I pinch the bridge of my nose and take a deep breath. *Calm down. There's no use panicking. I haven't done anything wrong.*

"Drive up to the gate and give our names. He said they should let us through." I whisper. Buck nods, and we roll up to the guard post. He rolls down the window and smiles at the guard.

"Name and license." The armed guard has a gruff voice. For a moment, he reminds me of Miller, with those dark sunglasses that conceal the soul like the windows of Huson Labs.

"Morning!" Buck grins and passes the guard his license. I fish my driver's permit out of my wallet and pass it to him. *What if they don't take permits? What if it's expired?*

Buck clears his throat. "Beautiful weather we're having, right?"

The guard doesn't respond. He takes the licenses and glances them over, then bends to peer into the car. I try to smile, but I can feel my lips wavering like Jell-O.

"State your purpose." The guard passes the licenses back. Buck glances at me.

"V-visiting family. Sebastian Brown…" I fiddle with my seat-belt, pulling it taut against my stomach.

"Science is pretty cool, right?" Buck asks. The guard doesn't acknowledge Buck. Instead, he turns to the computer inside his station and begins typing. I watch his fingers stab the keyboard. My hands feel slick with sweat. Buck reaches over and puts a hand on my knee. I try to take a breath. The guard stays where he is, then unclips the radio on his belt and brings it to his mouth. I swear my heart stops. He mutters something into the static that I can't make out. I hold my breath.

Then the gate in front of us buzzes and swings open.

"Building C," the guard says.

"Thanks!" Buck calls, and we drive through. I peer out the window and force myself to take a deep breath.

In front of Building A is a fountain in a courtyard. Benches and lush greenery surround it. Behind that, there's a gazebo with tables. If a guard with a gun hadn't just buzzed us in, I'd think it a nice place to picnic. Each bench, table, and walkway is empty, not a person in sight.

"Something doesn't feel right," Buck whispers. I nod as we continue to drive through the compound. Building C is in the back. It's different than Buildings A and B. There are no fountains back here, no picnic tables. Instead, big black vans are parked in rows. This building is *literally* built into the side of the mountain. The rocks jut out around the sides of the man-made structure, like nature reached out to take a bite of science, only to choke with it halfway lodged in its throat.

Two guards patrol the outside of this building. They've got pistols on their hips.

"'Huson Labs, Building C,'" Buck reads as we park. He slips the car keys into his pocket and attempts to give me a grin. I watch the front of the building as two glass doors open and Uncle Sebastian walks out.

"Okay," Buck whispers. "Remind me the plan?"

I suck in a breath. "Get in, get the tachyons, get out."

"And if Sebastian refuses to give them to us?"

I shrug. "We'll figure it out."

Buck shakes his head and unbuckles. "Great plan."

I step out of the car, and before I can shut the door, Uncle Sebastian is in front of me, wrapping me in a hug.

"Look at how big you are!" he crows, and I feel my cheeks heat. I pat him gently on the arm, and he steps back, grinning.

He's older than I remember him being. Gray hair hides in the edges of his inky black mane. His hair is long, coming down to his shoulders. He's tied it back into a loose ponytail. Stubble dots his chin, and behind his thick glasses, dark circles hang under his eyes. My heart aches. The last time I remember seeing him was before the accident. He had dark circles under his eyes then, too.

Buck walks around the side of the car and leans against the hood. Uncle Seb walks forward and shakes his hand.

"And you must be Buck. Great to meet you—George says you're a good kid."

Buck smiles. "I try."

"So," Uncle Seb claps his hands together. "Your dad says you're interested in quantum physics or the computer sciences—that you want to become a researcher here."

I nod and look away. "That's right."

Seb grins. "Takin' after your parents, I see. Well, no matter what you end up choosing, don't worry about anything. I'll take care of it all—art school, science school—it's taken care of, no matter what!"

"Wow." Buck's eyebrows shoot up into his hairline. "That's really generous."

Seb nods. "A promise is a promise," he says cryptically. He rubs his hands together and nods toward Building C. "Why don't we take a look inside?"

Nineteen

I HATE SCIENCE. REALLY. Doesn't matter what kind. If it requires any critical thinking or brainpower, I'm out. I flunked out of chemistry and biology in school and have struggled through math my entire life. You'd think math and science should be easy for me, given my genetics. I once asked my dad for math help when I was in seventh grade. He'd tried to teach me calculus instead, because "it's far more interesting than fractions."

I never asked for his help again.

Though, I think as Sebastian leads us through the building, rambling on and on about theory and equations, *now I wish I had asked again*. Because maybe if I had, I could get a word in edgewise with Uncle Seb. We've spent the past hour and a half touring the upper offices, then the lower offices, then—get this—the *middle* offices, and not *once* has there been an opportunity to talk about tachyons or time travel or *anything* important.

Uncle Seb leads us through another door, and we come out to a balcony overlooking the inner lobby. Glass panels act as railings for the balcony, which stretches the length of the room and ends in another doorway.

From here, I can see the security guards at the front desk. Buck nudges my arm and points to the ceiling. There, at the top, are big, circular, metal tubes.

"What's that?" I interrupt Uncle Seb's rambling and point up.

Uncle Seb's eyes follow my finger. "Oh, those are for security breaches. This whole building can lock down in just a couple of seconds! We've got an extremely high-grade security system in place here." Uncle Sebastian grins, then launches back into his sermon on science. I roll my eyes, turn away, and freeze.

Standing at the end of the hall is Miller.

I feel the air suck out of my lungs. For a second, it feels like the hallway is stretching, the walls around me growing bigger and bigger. I latch onto Buck's arm and tug. Miller is faced away from us. He's walking through another door. He hasn't seen us. *Or has he?*

"What?" Buck whispers and then looks where I'm looking. He inhales sharply—puts his arm around me.

"*Hey,* can we see your office?" Buck asks, voice just a pitch too high, smile strained. Uncle Sebastian pauses again.

"My office? I-I'm sorry, but my office isn't—"

"*Please*?" I step forward. Uncle Sebastian frowns. Then, he nods and pulls out his ID badge from his front pocket.

"Come with me," he says, and we walk back through the door we came through. I let out a breath, and together, Buck and I follow Uncle Seb down another hallway, then through another door. Already, I feel lost. I have no idea which direction we've gone—*how far we are from where we last saw Miller?*

Uncle Seb leads us through two large double doors, and the temperature drops. I wrap my arms around myself. The walls, floor, and ceiling are sterile white and the smell of hand sanitizer clings to the air. *It's suffocating in here.* All around us are tables with different types of equipment. Some things I can recognize from my dad's basement—others I've never seen before in my life.

Buck is staring past the equipment, his eyes wide and mouth stretched into a grin. Slowly, he points to a large computer in the corner.

"That's our pride and joy. We call it KELLY." Uncle Seb leads us over to the monitor. It's thick, with lots of lights and buttons on the front and sides. The computer itself is much taller than I am—taller even than Buck. I look at the monitor and see the letters: K-E-L-L-Y.

"She's how we run computer simulations—it's a specialized program we designed in-house to run the tests we do. Practice them before we perform them."

"So cool," Buck whispers. He reaches out, his fingers hovering just above the metal surface. Then, he shakes his head and yanks his arm back—shoves his fingers into his pocket.

"You're into computers?" Uncle Seb asks.

Buck nods. "You could say that."

I peer around Buck and look at his face. His eyes are shining. I can't understand the passion he has for tech, but the sight of him smiling is enough for me.

"He's got an interview Monday—Hyland Software, right?" I say.

"Really?" Uncle Seb sounds impressed. Buck rubs the back of his neck. Sebastian continues, "I know some guys who work there. I'll put in a good word for you."

"Really? You'd do that?" Buck's eyes widen.

"Of course!" Uncle Seb nods. Then he steps in front of the computer and starts typing. I glance over my shoulder at the door. Nobody's come in. Miller isn't in this room—*but he is here somewhere. We have to hurry. Get the tachyons and*—I stop as I catch sight of what's on the monitor.

"Is that—" I suck in a breath.

Uncle Seb nods. "Yep. The Tachyon Implementation of Mass and Energy. The TIME Machine... Do you want to watch this? I'd understand if—"

"Play it." I step closer. All sorts of information rapidly spawns on the screen. The machine is different—much different than what I'm used to. It's got to be an earlier design—an earlier model—than the one we have in the basement. I watch as a series of numbers runs along the right side of the screen, then a big red banner with the words "TEST UNSUCCESS-FUL" flashes. The image of the Machine changes, then more numbers and another failure. I lose count of how many failures we watch.

It's just like it is at home. Each one results in the same outcome.

What's that one quote? Being crazy means doing the same thing over, and over, and over again, expecting different results?

"Lorraine," Uncle Sebastian's voice is stern. I turn. His eyes are hard, his lips drawn down. "I know why you're actually here."

My throat catches my heart as it tries to make a violent escape from my body through my esophagus. I swallow. *Stay calm.*

"What do you mean?" I ask.

"You're here to learn more about her—your mother, Jessica."

I try to keep myself from exhaling a sigh of relief. I nod and look at the ground.

"Yeah," I whisper.

Uncle Seb puts his hand on my shoulder and squeezes. "Alright, then...come with me."

Twenty

WE FOLLOW SEBASTIAN through another set of double doors, down a flight of stairs, and finally to a looming elevator at the end of a sterile white hall.

"I'm not supposed to take guests down here but, given the topic of our conversation, privacy is a must," Uncle Seb explains. He pulls his keycard out of his pocket and presses it against the scanner on the wall. The green light at the top lights up, and I listen as the elevator rumbles from behind the two silver doors.

"Where are we going?" Buck asks. The elevator opens.

Uncle Seb steps through. "To the *real* lab." He turns on his heel, grinning, and stuffs his hands into his coat pockets. Buck and I hurry into the metal coffin, and the doors slide shut.

"I don't like this," Buck whispers as the elevator shifts and we descend. I can hear the groan of gears and realize, as I look at the number of floors this thing can go to, that we must be going underground. My heart hammers in my chest. I shut my eyes and try to picture what life will be like when this is all over—when we've saved Mom.

Mom... She'd *really* like Buck. He's so genuine, you can't *help* but like him. She'd probably take him to the field across from the house, show him her garden. Growing up, we'd sneak over to that abandoned field, to our secret pond. She and I planted strawberries there the summer before she... I hadn't ever gone back to keep up with the care, but Mom used to dutifully water and weed that garden until we had enough strawberries to have desserts for the rest of the summer.

The elevator stops with a *ding* and Uncle Seb pushes us out as the two doors slide open.

I follow Buck, who follows Uncle Seb. I keep close to him as I stare at the hallway around me. There isn't a single window down here, and the white fluorescent lights give the hallway a sterile feel. Like someone took a bottle of bleach and scrubbed each surface until their hands bled. We pass two large gray doors with a card reader lodged in the wall next to them, then take a left into another long hallway.

"What is this place?" I ask as we stop in front of a gray door.

Uncle Seb once again pulls out his security access card. "Like I said, this is the real lab. Up there"—he points up—"is just theory and idea generation. Down here, we run those theories and tests to see if they work. Come on—you'll want to see this."

We walk through the door into a dark room. Uncle Seb steps to the side and flicks on the lights.

It's a small office space, with just three desks crammed together in the middle of the room.

"A bit unconventional, but they still haven't hired anybody for my department, so…" Uncle Seb trails off.

I walk toward the desk on the right. Papers are scattered around, with handwriting so messy that it's barely legible. Little sketches of hearts or random eyeballs are in the margins. I place my hand on the cool brown surface of the desk and my heart skips a beat.

"This was your mom's. Your dad's is to the right, and mine is the one on the left." Uncle Seb moves into the room, walks over to his desk, and sits with a sigh.

My eyes wander over to Dad's desk, and I press my lips together. Six blue vials of glowing liquid sit in the container on the right of it. Those have to be the tachyons Dad told us about.

"It's so…organized," Buck mutters. "I would have expected this from Lorraine's mom, not her dad."

Uncle Seb laughs. "Are you kidding? George was the most organized man on the planet! Her mom and I used to move his stuff around—not much, just a fraction of an inch—and time how long it would take him to notice. Used to drive him nuts."

I think about my dad's current workspace in the basement. Everything is strewn about down there, like a tornado had come through and then, for good measure, doubled back to really mess everything up. My room looked similar to my mom's desk. Things left right where I'd last used them.

I reach forward and grab a tube of ruby-red lipstick, holding it up to the light. It's like this desk is trapped in time. Just like my dad. Trapped in that moment.

"What's that?" Buck nods to Uncle Sebastian's desk. On a metal stand is a device. It looks like one of those handheld scanners you use at the grocery store to ring up items, except that on the back is a small screen with a big silver knob underneath it.

"Oh, that's a…special project I'm working on." Uncle Seb scratches the back of his neck. "Since the accident, I've shifted from studying time to studying the mind. It's supposed to help people recover their memories through specific flashing light patterns. You know, people who have Alzheimer's, dementia, amnesia—not trauma-induced amnesia, though…that one's, uh, *real* tough to crack."

Buck reaches for it, but Uncle Sebastian quickly steps forward.

"It's—not ready yet. We…got the light sequences to affect

memory, but…not *exactly* in the way we would've hoped." He clears his throat. "Memory is fascinating—the mind is, too. I've gotten to work on hundreds of different inventions that can help with behavior modification, memory aids—truly, it's a one of a kind opportunity."

"Right…" Buck cocks his head to the side. "So, what does it do then?"

"Uh…well, like I said, it will help restore memories…eventually…but, uh, right now it appears that it…does the opposite of that." Uncle Sebastian frowns.

I glance at the device. My memories, or lack thereof, are already the subject of great distress. I look down at the lipstick tube and roll it around my fingers.

"Your mom was a wild woman, Lorraine," Uncle Sebastian sighs. I pocket the tube and step around the desk to his side of the room. He turns to face me. I glance at the vials of tachyons, then up at Buck. It's now or never. I open my mouth—ready to ask him.

"Lorraine, be honest with me…" Sebastian is twiddling his thumbs together, eyes trained on the floor. "You aren't actually interested in quantum physics or research, are you…"

I look away. "No."

"Why are you here, then?"

I bite the inside of my cheek and shift. "I... Well—"

"Be honest with me, Lorrie," Uncle Sebastian whispers.

I look up and meet his eyes. *Be honest?* "I *want* my *mom* back."

The words pierce the room. As if we're standing in an oxygen chamber, all the air wooshes out and we're left in the suffocating silence. Buck's eyes dart from me, to Sebastian, then, back to me again. I'm a bug under a microscope, pierced by the gaze of the so-called scientists around me, pinning me down, trying to figure out what makes me tick. I shift, swallow, but refuse to break.

Uncle Sebastian finally nods. "And you think time travel is the way to do that." It isn't a question. I nod anyway.

Uncle Seb sighs and leans back in his chair. It squeaks. He folds his hands over his stomach. "Lorraine...what has your dad actually told you about that night? About the night of the test?"

I shrug. "Not much. I know I was there."

Uncle Sebastian nods. "You were... Do you remember anything?"

I shake my head.

"Your mom and dad were...passionate about the Machine. So passionate that they secretly built one in their basement to conduct experiments in their off-time. These... Lorraine, we had no idea they were running these experiments. The night of the accident, you'd had a nightmare, so you went downstairs right as the test had started... Your dad left that room for just a second to get you back upstairs and then—"

"He's told me that much." I can't speak above a whisper. Something is lodged in my throat. It aches, bringing a sting to my eyes. Uncle Seb tilts his head to the side.

"By the time he got back, the Machine was out of control, and your mom was trapped inside. It...wasn't pretty... Did he tell you my working theory on that particular experiment?"

I lean against the wall and cross my arms. "No. He didn't."

Uncle Sebastian nods. He leans back in his chair and stares up at the fluorescent lights. "Time travel is impossible. There just isn't enough energy in the world—tachyon or no tachyon. I think that the energy we harnessed burst right out of the Machine when it malfunctioned, and..." He pauses, then stands. He shoves his hands into his white pockets. I look up at him. "Lorraine, the readings of radiation were unlike anything we've ever seen, and...well, what was left of your mom..."

My throat starts to burn. "What are you saying?"

"I'm saying that if any time traveling *did* happen that night, your mom wouldn't have been alive to see it. The burst of radiation would have killed her in a nanosecond." Uncle Seb put his hand on my shoulder. I look away, past him, to the blue vials of tachyons on my dad's desk—and I freeze.

One's missing.

I look up at Buck, who has his hands shoved deep in his pockets, his lips pressed together. He nods his head toward Uncle Sebastian and reaches for another vial.

The room spins. I reach my hand to the wall and balance against the concrete, then force myself to look back at Uncle Seb. *Did he notice?* My eyes burn, and panic claws at my throat. I see Buck swipe another vial and shove it into his hoodie pocket. Uncle Sebastian squeezes my shoulder and I look back into his eyes.

"Time travel is dangerous, Lorraine. You can't mess with it, okay?"

"But aren't *you* still experimenting with it?" my voice quakes as I speak. "I-if *you* can, why can't I?"

"I'm *not*, Lorraine," Uncle Sebastian's voice takes a hard tone. He shakes his head. "Huson discontinued all experimentation on the Machine once your mom died. It...was just too dangerous. Even we can recognize that. Mrs. Huson even visited your dad herself to talk to him about it. I mean—your dad's lucky they didn't press charges, that he didn't get tried for leaking top secret information, or for endangering you—*a child.* Lorraine, if Huson Labs hadn't stepped in, you would've been taken from your father, put in the system... He would have gone to jail." Uncle Sebastian sighs. He rubs his hand over his face and takes a half-step back, his body turning away.

Buck's reaching for another vial.

I panic. "I can't—I can't stop. It's...the *only* thing my dad cares about."

Uncle Sebastian turns back to me. "He *cares* about *you*."

"He cares about the Machine!" the shout rips itself from my throat. Buck's hand hesitates over the last vial for a moment, and he looks up. Then, he swipes it and stuffs it into his pocket. He steps away from the desk and leans against the door.

"Lorraine," Uncle Seb whispers. His eyes are dripping with pity. I feel like a kettle about to boil over, my cheeks are hot and tears are threatening to leak from my eyes. I suck a breath in through my nose and then slowly force it out through my mouth.

"Whatever—*never mind*," I huff. I cross my arms tightly over my chest. Uncle Sebastian sighs. He runs a hand over his face, then looks up and meets my eyes.

"Lorraine, the Machine is dangerous...too dangerous to keep looking into. Just...please, promise me you'll stop trying to time travel."

My heart beats in my ears. I nod and look away. My lips waver. "Okay."

I hear Uncle Seb let out a sigh of relief. Then he's patting my shoulder and turning toward Buck. "I think that concludes our tour for the day. Come on, let me walk you two out."

I let Uncle Sebastian guide us back through the maze of the lab. Buck is next to me, his hands resting in his pocket, stance relaxing, face light. I sniff and wipe my eyes. Then I wrap my arm around his, and together we walk three vials of pure-blue, tachyon-infused liquid up through the elevator, down the hall, and, finally, out of Building C.

Time travel is "dangerous"? Yeah, right. If I could do it when I was twelve, what was stopping me from doing it now? *Screw Sebastian. Screw Huson Labs.* I slide into the passenger seat. As Buck pulls out of the parking spot, I wave goodbye to Uncle Seb. I keep my eye on the cars around us—looking for Miller or his silver sedan. We're silent, tense, as we drive past the security gate and back onto the open road.

"Oh, thank God." I collapse in my seat as we drive further and further away from the building. "I can't *believe* we just did that."

"Lorraine, was that true, what you were saying in there?" Buck asks. I look up at him, raising a brow. He continues, "A-about the Machine and what your dad cares about."

I look away. "I had to distract him—so *you* could grab those vials. Nice thinking, by the way. There was *no way* he was going to *willingly* give them to us after *that* disaster of a conversation."

"What's your dad going to think of me?" Buck whispers. He's gripping the steering wheel hard, his knuckles white. I reach over and rub his shoulder.

"We won't tell him. We'll just say Uncle Seb gave them to us, and that he warned us not to speak about it—that Huson Labs was listening in on his phone."

"We'll see," he whispers. We settle into a silence that sticks around for the rest of the drive home.

Twenty-One

I STAND NEXT TO THE CHARRED METAL MACHINE and trace a finger in the soot. Dad has done wonders to it. The basic frame is back in place with fresh tubes connecting to it, pumping the strange glowing tachyons through the pipes. The metal is cool to the touch and leaves a black smudge on my finger. I take a step back and shove my hands in my pockets, gripping the tube of ruby-red lipstick.

"Hey—Mr. Sullivan!" Buck calls from the computer monitor. Buck's fingers fly over the keyboard. His eyebrows scrunch together.

"What's up, Buck?" Dad moves the welder mask away from his face and pops up from inside the Machine. I step away and slip past the safety shield, then walk up just behind Buck.

If I can't understand the science of time travel, what made me think I could ever do what Lorrie was doing? Then again, maybe the science of it doesn't really matter. If understanding time travel was what gave you the ability to travel through time, my dad should have been able to figure it out ages ago, right?

Behind me, my dad walks up and stares at the screen. He slings his arm around my shoulder and leans forward.

"Oh—no, that's fine, Buck. It always looks like that before a test. The natural radiation in the air around us gets all stirred up. The higher those readings, the better our chance of a successful test—just like the one you and Lorraine ran, actually." He looks at me, grinning. His eyes seem to hold a light that I realize I haven't seen in a while. The last time I'd caught my dad smiling like that had been before the accident.

I can see it—for the first time in a long time, *I can finally see it. Us, together, happy again.*

Dad stands with his hand on my shoulder as he turns back to the Machine, prattling on about science I don't care to understand. I swallow past the sudden lump in my throat, and I lean my head against his shoulder. *We can be happy again—once Mom is back, it could be like this, us together, forever.* What else my future can hold—*university, a better job*—it doesn't matter. *I can think about all those once I have Mom.*

"Now!" My dad rubs his hands together. "The ethics of time travel, from the top!"

"Stay on the trail," I say.

Buck squares his shoulders. "Leave whatever you find."

Dad's smile widens. "Respect the wildlife—and?"

Buck and Dad speak at the same time, but I find I have no words to join them as they say, "Time is fixed—*don't play God!*"

Dad's fingers clack on the keyboard, then he moves to the control panel and pulls a lever.

Around us, gears moan as the generator comes to life. I stare at the Machine and I realize that a small, secret part of me wishes I could understand how it works. *What makes time travel so accessible from a hunk of metal?* Only the greatest minds can understand, and unfortunately for me, I'm not on that list.

The Machine spins around and around. I focus on the top of the Machine, watching as the metal begins to heat, glowing a burnt auburn color. I can feel a wave of heat waft off of it, breaking against the plastic barrier like the ocean against the beach.

And just like that, a memory flashes across my eyes.

I was standing on the basement stairs, staring at that orange metal on the top of the Machine. It glowed. Blue electric arches of lightning shot out from the Machine. I saw a figure inside the churning metal, holding...something. Across the room, my father typed furiously on the keyboard, no plastic safety shield in sight. I walked down the stairs as if in a trance, closer to the light—a moth to the flame. I held my stuffed tiger, Bean, in my arms. My toes curled as I touched the cold concrete of the basement floor. My hair was tied back in a braid and I could feel the end wriggling and writhing in the wind.

Someone calls my name—my *full* name—and then I'm back in reality.

Buck's hand is on my shoulder. He stares at me, his eyebrows scrunched together like someone's tied a string through them and gathered them up like fabric.

"Lorraine, are you okay?" he asks. I nod. He squints, leaning toward me. "Are you sure?"

I nod again. I remembered something. *Finally.* I pat Buck on the arm and let out a breath. "I'm fine."

I look at the Machine as the metal arms begin to spin faster, faster, faster—watch as they spin so fast I can hardly see them anymore. The lights above us pulse with energy.

A ball of light forms in the middle of the Machine. I gasp. My dad hasn't stopped grinning.

"It's working!" He jostles my shoulders as he jumps in the air. "It's working!"

There's a blue light shining in the Machine's core, small lightning bolts of electricity spurting and shooting away from it. Then another wave of heat. The light bursts from the Machine's center and wafts through the room. Despite the plastic shield, my hair ruffles. I gasp—the air around me is warm and muggy. It crawls through my nose and into my lungs like sludge. The lights flicker. Energy pulses in the air.

"*Remember*, Lorraine," I whisper to myself, forcing myself to focus on the orange metal on the top of the Machine. I can imagine how it must sizzle from the pure energy cascading around it. I squint. "Remember!"

All of us stand behind the shield, watching intently as the TIME Machine continues to whir, to pick up energy. This is the farthest a test has ever gotten—the closest we've ever been!

And then, out of the corner of my eye something pulls at my attention.

The air changes, a wave of heat wafts toward me, and Lorrie appears in a brilliant blue zap of electricity.

The air is sucked from my lungs. *What is she doing here?* She's too close to the Machine. Horror and dread grip my chest like ice as I see my dad shift. He steps closer to the shield, his hand pressed against the plastic. Then, in a second, he slips out from the safety wall and runs toward Lorrie.

"Dad!" I shriek, then turn to Buck. "Turn it off—turn it off!"

Buck types furiously on the keyboard. I watch, safe behind the shield, as Lorrie steps closer to the Machine, then even closer. My dad races after her, struggling past pipes and wires.

The air around me shifts again, and the hair on the back of my neck rises. There's another burst of heat from the Machine and I watch as my dad holds his hands in front of his face. Lorrie is standing close—too close—her hair whipping wildly around her face. She's standing on the tips of her toes, her shoulders hunched. Then, as my dad finally reaches her, she shifts out of the way and drives her shoulder into his side, shoving him toward the Machine.

I watch her movements—watch in horror as she moves as if she's practiced this a thousand times. Like she'd been trying to lure him out here, to the Machine, to shove him into the belly of the beast.

My dad falls forward. It's like time is moving slower now. I'm not sure if it's my perception of things or if it's the Machine. I can't move any faster, even though I try to get out from the shield—to get to my dad before he's sucked inside, before he can vanish from my life like Mom did.

But then his foot catches a pipe and he falls on his knees, face inches from the whirring mechanical arms.

He scrambles away, yanking at the pipes. There's a burst of power. Electric sparks spit from the Machine as a cord comes unplugged. The lights flicker. There's one final burst of heat, then the Machine's arms begin to slow.

"It's off!" Buck cheers. "I turned it off!"

I stalk around the safety shield, across the room, and grab Lorrie by the wrist.

"What were you *thinking*?" I shout in her face. She turns to me, her eyes welling with tears, and she grits her teeth together.

"It didn't *work*!" her shriek echoes off the concrete walls. She stomps her foot. "You promised it would work if we got his help! You're a liar! You lied!" She screws her eyes shut, her face red, as she continues to shriek, "Liar—liar—liar!"

She wrenches her hand out of my grasp and stomps her foot again.

"What were you trying to do?!" I demand. "Why? Why did you push him?!"

Her shrieks drown out my accusations. I look past her to my dad. He's lying on the floor, his feet tangled in the pipes and wires. His glasses have slid down his nose as he stares at Lorrie, his jaw slack.

"My God," he whispers. My stomach twists into a tight knot. I feel like I'm trapped on top of a mountain—one wrong step in either direction and I'm tumbling into an abyss far below.

"Dad—it's not what you think." I step around Lorrie, my hands up. "She… I-I—"

He scrambles to his feet and takes three quick steps around me.

Before I can stop him, he's grabbed Lorrie by the shoulders and spins her around to face him.

Her shouts die in her throat, her mouth still open as she stares up at him. Her eyes widen and tears slip down her round, freckled cheeks.

"You're—" she cuts herself off as Dad wraps her in a hug and closes his eyes.

"I'm sorry—" he cuts himself off with a sob. My gut drops. Big, fat tears leak from his eyes. They dribble down his cheeks and collect on top of Lorrie's head. My dad's shoulders tremble as he holds her—his daughter, young and innocent—tight against his chest. "I'm so sorry."

Lorrie pushes against his stomach. She writhes in his grasp, finds her voice. "Let go of me! You—let go of me!"

Dad releases his grip, and she stumbles back.

"I hate you!" she shrieks. The venom in her words stings like a snakebite. Dad recoils.

Lorrie points a slender finger like a dagger at my dad's chest. She clenches her teeth together. "I wish it had been *you* in her place!"

And then she turns and races up the stairs. The sound of the basement door slamming shut a second later echoes through the room. I close my eyes. My heart, like a bird trapped inside a house, flutters wildly in my chest.

"Is that true?" my dad whispers. I shake my head numbly. Words escape me.

"She's...just a kid," I finally whisper. "I didn't—she doesn't know any better."

"But she's here." Dad looks up now, and for the first time I notice how tired his eyes are. Have they always looked like that?

Dad looks away, shaking his head. "Why didn't you tell me?"

I cross my arms. "She told me not to."

"And you listened to her?" Dad's voice rises in pitch.

I shove my nose in the air, popping my hip to the side as I sneer. "Yes, I did. Because out of everyone in this room, she's the only one who has *actually* traveled through time—"

"She's *twelve!*" My dad shouts, and I flinch. Buck wraps his arm around me. Dad continues. "She's twelve, and she's grieving! She just lost her mom, and you think she knows what's best for herself? For everyone?"

"What was I *supposed* to *do?*" I take a step forward—push Buck away from me.

"Tell me!" My dad pounds his chest. "You should have told me! Trusted me to be your father—"

"You lost that right!" There's no going back now. Just like that, the dam is broken, and the words I'd spoken only in hushed whispers to a video camera late at night come rushing out. "You *lost* my trust! You put science and-and time travel before your family—before your wife! *You killed her*! You killed her and you took her from me and-and-and you expect me to be able to forgive you for that?"

My dad doesn't look hurt. He doesn't look at me with wide-eyed pain or any sense of my words landing in his heart. He stares at me, his eyes narrowed, his lips pulled into a tight line. His jaw is clenched.

I can't breathe—no matter how many heaving breaths I suck into my lungs, the room still spins and my lungs still burn. His reservation pokes at my heart. It makes me seethe. *He should be sorry—he should feel guilty!* Instead, he stands there as if he'd expected these hateful words to leave my mouth. As if I hadn't done everything in my power to keep the peace between us all these years.

As if this is all *my* fault.

"I can't," I whisper. "I can't do it. I can't—you broke our family. You *took* my *mom*...and no matter what you say, I'm going to get her back."

I stalk toward the basement stairs but stop when I reach the landing. I stare down at my dad. He watches me with that quiet reservation—like he's biding his time. Buck stands still, caught between looking at me and my dad.

"I'm going to go get Lorrie. I'm going to bring her back here. We're going to save Mom—*with or without you,*" I hiss.

My dad shakes his head. "*Lorrie,* our family—"

"Died the day Mom did."

I turn and bolt up the basement stairs two at a time. When I reach the top, I turn and throw all my strength into slamming the door shut behind me. I know where Lorrie is going. I haven't been back there in ages, and I dread seeing it again...but I can't let her go there alone.

Twenty-Two

I DASH ACROSS THE STREET and toward the abandoned field. The sky above me is dark. I pull out my phone and click on the flashlight, the white light guiding me. I pick my way through tall grass and try not to think about the ticks.

I jump over the ditch, duck under a tree, and come to a dilapidated, chicken wire fence. Mom had cut the wires a long time ago, and a tangle of foliage has sort of taken over. The metal poles are rusted, and a bush took residence in front of the hole, but I suck in a breath and manage to squeeze my way through.

The dirt under my sneakers is hard and cracked. I scan the path for footprints anyway. A patch of grass trampled here. A twig snapped there.

Finally, I come around a bush and stop in a small clearing.

The pond's gone. That shouldn't shock me, but it does. In its place is a dried-up indent of the earth. The bushes around us are covered in weeds, not a strawberry in sight. Lorrie is sitting on the ground at the bank of the dried-up pond, her legs to her chest and her chin tucked behind her knees.

"Lorrie..." I take a step toward her. I can't ask if she's okay—I know that she's not. I can't find the energy to shout or condemn her. *This is a mess—a disaster.* I can't remember any of this, the traveling in time, trying to save my mom. I can't even remember what it was like in those first few years without her.

I square my shoulders and walk until I'm standing next to her. She sniffles, shifts away. I sit next to her and bring my legs to my chest. I rest my chin on my knees and stare at the dried-up pond.

We sit in silence, the night stretching on around us. I hear a cricket in the bushes, and I can imagine him playing a tiny, pitiful violin for our pitiful problems.

"The pond's gone," Lorrie whispers. I put my arm around her shoulder.

"Yep," I whisper back. "Sucks...doesn't it?"

Lorrie sniffs again—she wipes her nose with the back of her hand. "Yeah..."

I frown. "But that's just life, isn't it...things change. Ponds dry up. Strawberry bushes get overgrown."

"We should come back and fill it with water," Lorrie whispers.

"If we just tried—filled it every couple days—made sure that it stayed full...it wouldn't dry up."

I look at her—really look at her. She seems so tiny next to me. Thin arms, dark circles under her eyes. Her hair needs to be washed. I wonder how long ago it's been, for her, since Mom died. She doesn't have her panda-bear purse anymore. Just jeans and a black hoodie. She isn't wearing the sparkling clip-on earrings or the Silly Bandz. She looks different from the last time I saw her. Skinnier. Darker.

She looks more like me.

"Lorrie, it's just a pond..." I pick at a crack in the dirt and watch as it flakes beneath my fingers. "These things...they just happen..."

Her face contorts into a scowl. She picks up a loose stone and chucks it at the weed-covered strawberry bushes. "Why are you here?"

I frown and lean back on my hands. "Someone has to take care of you."

Lorrie stands, her fists balled at her side. I watch as she opens her mouth, then closes it again. She turns away, her arms crossed.

"If you really cared for me," she whispers, "you'd help me save my mom. If you cared for me, you'd care for her."

It's my turn to scowl. "I do care for her, Lorrie."

She whirls around to face me. Tears stream down her cheeks. "No, no you don't! You care more about Dad and doing things his way than you care about Mom—if you really loved her, you'd drop everything to get even one more second with her."

I jump to my feet, towering over her. Anger like fire ants crawls through my veins. "You don't think I haven't prayed every day of my life that things would be different? For Mom to come back? Well guess what, Lorrie, I have—*and it hasn't happened*!"

"But it can!" Lorrie cried. "It can if you would just—"

Bright hot light lights up our surroundings. I gasp and look back at the house. Blue lightning cracks up from the ground. It zigzags through the sky in a blinding flash and connects with a cloud, then the world returns to darkness. Seconds later, a thunderous boom shakes the ground. Lorrie shrieks and slaps her hands over her ears.

"Buck," I whisper. *Buck is back there.* Then, I'm running back through the bushes and trees, back down the path. I'm running—running away from the dried-up pond and away from Lorrie.

Twenty-Three

A SCREAM LURCHES from my throat. "Buck!"

I squeeze through the cut-out in the fence.

"Buck!"

"Lorraine?!"

I hear him—I look around wildly and dash around the tree. Buck stands fifteen feet away, his hair covered in leaves. There's a tear on the sleeve of his jacket. I race toward him.

"Buck—what happened to your arm? Are you hurt?" I pull at the tear to look at the skin. Buck swats my hand away.

"I'm fine. I was trying to find you but got stuck on a thorn—what was that light?"

We both look at the house.

"Dad." Dread is stagnant water in my stomach. "Dad—the Machine—Oh, Buck, what have we done?"

Buck squeezes me into a hug, then slides his hand into mine.

Together, we jump across the ditch and run up the street.

Right in front of my house, in the driveway, the lights flashing, is a police officer's patrol car. The big, black Huson vans are parked at the neighbor's house. I dig my heels into the asphalt and yank Buck's arm.

"Lorr—"

"Miller!" I hiss. Buck notices the vans then. We slip behind a scraggle of bushes and watch the front of my house. The doors are wide open but the lights remain off.

"Why are the doors open—did you shut the doors?" I whisper. Buck swallows and shakes his head.

"I-I don't remember."

I hold my breath as we watch the front of the house. Suddenly, all the lights flicker back on. Power returns to the house, the streetlamps, and the entire neighborhood. I hadn't realized that whatever had happened had taken the power for the whole block with it.

Miller steps out of the front door. He takes off his sunglasses—scans the street. Buck and I hold still, like we're hiding from a masked killer in the woods. I can almost picture a hockey mask and chainsaw in Miller's hand. Miller holds up his hand and walks toward one of the black vans.

Moments later, three men in black uniforms step out of the

house, my father between them. They guide him, in handcuffs, toward the black van and slide open the door. My dad climbs in... The door slams like the lid of a coffin.

I stand—to grab him, to bring him back, I don't know. Buck snatches my wrist and pulls me back down.

"Buck—"

He presses his finger to my lips. Then he points to the front door. More men file out of the house. Like ants swarming the carcass of a deer hit by a semi, they flood in and out of my home. They're searching through it, crossing it off with yellow police tape.

"*Lorraine.*" Buck inches back. He tugs my wrist. "*Lorraine, we have to go.*"

I watch as they swarm around my home. I imagine them picking through my room, going through the whole house. I imagine them invading the basement, finding the Machine—*they'd take the Machine.* They'd dismantle it and take it, and I'd never be able to save my mom—*I'm never going to be able to fix this.*

I press my hand over my mouth to stop the sob from escaping, and let Buck drag me away from home, away from my life, and away from everything I know.

Twenty-Four

WE WALK FOREVER, in the dark, like two refugees sneaking across the border. My feet ache by the time we slow from a run to a jog, then a jog to a walk. It's humid. I've swatted away about a thousand mosquitoes. I don't even know where we're walking to or why—there's no plan. Not anymore.

We're just trying to get as far away as we can.

We're on a side street, miles from home. We pass houses I don't recognize as we walk farther and farther. The ache goes from my heels up into my shins.

A silver sedan speeds through a cross street in front of us— Buck and I freeze, then duck behind a set of trash cans. We're silent, barely breathing, until we're sure he won't double back— until we're positive that we're safe, for now.

Buck lets out a breath and sits on the curb. He hangs his head and runs a hand over his face.

"*Oh God*, Lorraine, we're fugitives," he whispers. "We're fugitives."

I close my eyes and tilt my head up to the awakening sky. *This is a disaster.*

"What do we do?" I whisper. I wish my dad were here. Despite everything, despite all we'd said and done to each other, I wish it were him sitting next to me on the curb. That he'd tell me what to do already so I wouldn't have to worry about it. That he'd have a plan to save the TIME Machine, to go back, to get Mom. I frown and look at my lap... What would he do?

The idea strikes like that strange bolt of lightning that'd struck my house. I reach into my pocket and yank out my phone.

"Who are you calling?" Buck asks.

I press a contact I've called only once before. I put the phone to my ear and wait as I listen to it ring. Then, finally, it picks up.

"Uncle Seb," I whisper. "We need your help."

Twenty-Five

UNCLE SEB SENT A CAR. It's a luxury black sedan. I know it's luxury because when Buck and I climb in the back, there's a box of snacks in a built-in cooler. The seats are tan leather. The driver, a muscly man with a scar on his left chin, doesn't care to ask us who we are.

He waits until the door closes and then pulls away from the curb.

There's light jazz music playing on the radio. I can't hear the engine of the car or the way it rumbles over the road. The car, the snacks—all of it is a level of perfection I've never known—that I never even dreamed of knowing.

My stomach rolls. Buck helps himself to the crackers in the cooler but I turn my head to stare out the window. *I don't belong among the pretty things of life.*

In a little over half an hour, we glide off the freeway, take a few turns down some side streets, then come to a concrete drive-way. Thick trees surround it, the branches reaching out into the path with their scratchy limbs—like those trees from the old *Snow White* cartoon. Dread pools in my stomach.

The car slows and our driver presses a button. The gate swings open and we drive through. We're taken up a hill. Perfect little lamps along the ground light the way. Finally, we come around a corner and see the house.

Buck leans forward, a half-eaten cracker dropping from his mouth and onto the floor. I wince. *There are crumbs everywhere.*

"Babe—"

Buck grabs my hand and points to the house.

Which isn't a house at all.

It's a mansion.

Three stories of modern architecture. Surrounding the home are sprawling gardens. We pass a fountain—a cupid shooting wa-ter from the tip of his bow—and a distant memory knocks. I feel like I used to run through those gardens. It goes as quickly as it comes, like it's trapped behind a thick plastic shield.

We pull up to the front of the house, underneath a large black marble awning. It feels like we're entering a cave or a secret lair.

"Is your uncle secretly Batman?" Buck whispers. "Or Lex Luthor?"

I shake my head. I don't know.

Uncle Sebastian is on the white marble steps. He's not wearing the lab coat we'd previously seen him in. Instead, he's got brown corduroy pants and a dark purple turtleneck sweater. Uncle Sebastian's hair is slicked back into a ponytail and he's holding a crystal glass of what looks to be whisky. The car rolls to a stop and the driver parks.

"Thank you," I mutter to the driver. He ignores me, staring straight ahead. I shake my head and slip out of the car. Buck follows, and I shut the door with my hip.

The moment we're out, the car pulls away and vanishes back down the driveway. It's just us now. Me, Buck, and Uncle Sebastian.

"*In-side,*" Uncle Sebastian pronounces each syllable of the word as though it physically pains him. His teeth are clenched, his eyes turned into slits. "*Now.*"

I hug myself tight as Uncle Sebastian turns on his heel and stalks through the big front doors—I'm not sure what they're made of, but whatever it is, it looks expensive. They're tall, black as night with silver handles. Buck and I follow Uncle Seb into the home. The air is cold in there. I wrap my hands around my forearms and look at the ground. White-and-black tile floor, like we're on a life-size chessboard.

Uncle Sebastian leads us through the manor. I feel like a woman being brought to trial. *Is there a noose waiting for me at the end of all this?*

We stop in a hallway. I glance out the window. The sun starts to rise, the sky turning from midnight black to misty gray. Uncle Sebastian is looking down at his phone. I can hear it vibrate every few seconds, the screen lighting up with a new message or notification.

"Uncle Seb?" I ask. His brow furrows. He brings his crystal cup to the edge of his lips—hesitates for a second—then sighs and brings it away. He shoves the phone into his pocket.

"It's late," he says. He finally turns to look at me. I watch as he tries to smile. He drags a hand over his eyes. "Come. I'll show you to a guest bedroom... We can sort this out in a few hours."

I nod, even though I know I won't be able to sleep—not with everything that's happened. Not with everything that could still happen.

I try to think of something—anything—other than my dad behind iron bars. He wouldn't be able to take his weekly walks in prison. I'm not sure why, but it's that thought that brings a sting to my eyes. I swallow, smooth my palms on my jeans. Uncle Seb leads us down another sterile white-and-black hallway.

"Here we go, Buck. You can sleep in this one." Uncle Seb

motions to a gray door. Buck nods, kisses the top of my forehead, then slips inside. Uncle Sebastian continues down the hall and I follow silently. He stops at another gray door. I reach for the handle, pausing when Uncle Sebastian clears his throat.

I look up at him. He's staring at the ground. His lips are trembling.

I open my mouth, but no words come out. It's like they're caught, held back by an invisible hand that's reached out and wrapped its fingers around my throat.

Sebastian looks up at me. His eyes are full of unshed tears.

"Is"—his breath hitches partway through his sentence—"he alive?"

I nod. "Yes," I whisper. "Dad's alive."

Uncle Sebastian lets out a shuddery breath. He nods, pats my shoulder, then turns and stumbles down the hall. "Good-night, Lorrie."

My gut twists. A knife is lodged in my heart. I slip through the bedroom door without saying a word.

Twenty-Six

IT TAKES ME HOURS TO FALL ASLEEP. My heart races along with my thoughts all through the night. I toss and turn in the queen-size, four-poster bed. I try to keep my eyes shut and let sleep take me, but every time I close my eyes, a memory flashes before them.

I'd seen a figure in the Machine... It had to have been my mom. She was inside the Machine, those metal arms spinning wildly around her.

Her back had been turned to me in the memory. What had she been looking at? Whatever it was, that's the key to getting her out of the Machine and back with me where she belongs.

She's trapped there—she can't get out by herself. Somewhere, back in the past, she's alive and breathing. *What if Mom's stuck in the seconds where we can't see her? Can't reach her?*

I roll over onto my side, shoving my face into a silky pillow.

My eyes grow heavy...my mind swims...

Then I'm standing in the basement of our house. I'm standing next to the Machine, the arms spinning madly. I can feel the wind rushing around me, the energy pulsing in the air. My mom's trying to step out, jumping back each time a metal arm swings around. I reach out—I brush her fingers—and then feel something in me shift. It's like I'm trapped inside my mind, watching someone else use my body, control my actions.

I watch my hand hesitate. Then it yanks back, away from my mom. My mom grabs for me, reaching out of the metal cage—only for her arm to snap in half as the metal limb swings around and crashes into her. She shrieks, a high-pitched tone. I hear her arm crack. I can see bone.

I'm abandoning her—I can't, I can't leave her—

My eyes snap open. Sunlight drifts through the large windows on my left. Even if it was just a dream, it stays with me, like a bullet between the ribs. I rub my eyes—they hurt. I must've only slept for a few hours.

I lay between the silk pillows and sheets, forcing my eyes closed to try and catch a few more hours of sleep. But it's like my brain is hooked up to a generator, my thoughts rushing faster and faster—so fast I can barely catch what it is I'm thinking. I grunt, pull myself up, and slip out of bed.

I stumble out of the bedroom, down the hall, and into the kitchen.

Uncle Sebastian is behind the stove, grilling pancakes. I blink.

"Good morning." Uncle Sebastian waves as I hesitate. I nod, then force myself to shuffle forward.

In the morning light, the manor is even fancier—even more perfect—that it had been the night before. The kitchen is an open concept, with a breakfast nook to my right and a couple of couches to my left. Taking up the entire left side of the wall are floor-to-ceiling windows. I know it's morning because of the light outside, but I can't see the sun—not with the thick forest up against the large glass panes.

I approach the kitchen bar, slipping onto a pitch-black seat.

Uncle Seb sets a plate of pancakes in front of me, then moves back to grilling. I look down at them. They're burnt.

"Do you remember when you'd come to stay here?" Uncle Sebastian asks. He keeps his face turned away from me. His hair has fallen out of its ponytail. He's in the same clothes as he was yesterday. I see a tightness in his shoulders. I wonder if he slept last night.

"No," I whisper. "When did I do that?"

He shakes his head. "Lots of times—especially after your mom passed. Sometimes your dad just…needed a break, so I'd watch you. I'd make you pancakes, and we'd draw together... You had so many questions back then, about time travel. You were so curious about what happened. Angry too."

"Oh," I whisper. I don't know what else to say. I look down at the pancakes and ask, "Did you burn the pancakes back then, too?"

Uncle Sebastian turns now to glare at me. "No. It's just... It's been a while."

I nod, pour some syrup out of a glass, and silently eat. Uncle Seb continues to flip the pancakes and set them on a dish. They get less and less burnt as he works, and I can't help but feel I got the short end of the stick here.

"Morning," Buck calls from the hallway. He shuffles into the kitchen. His clothes are rumpled, and he's got the worst case of bedhead that I've seen in a while. I don't know how, but Buck makes it work. He's cute like this. He pats my back and then presses a kiss against my cheek. Uncle Seb sets a plate of pancakes down next to me, then turns off the stove and dusts off his hands.

"Right," he says, then turns to look at me. The bags under his eyes are a dark shade of purple. He *definitely* didn't sleep last night. "Eat up, then join me in the study. We have to talk."

My stomach twists. I feel like a child with their hand caught in a cookie jar. Buck shrugs and digs into the pancakes. I push my plate away, a frown weighing me down. I'm not hungry anymore.

Twenty-Seven

UNCLE SEBASTIAN STANDS with his arms crossed. "You stole the tachyons."

It's a statement. Final. Unwavering and stained with a hint of disappointment.

I'm standing in the study, squirming under Uncle Sebastian's hard, cold gaze. On one end of the room is Uncle Sebastian's dark oak desk. It faces us, and if it had eyes they would be just as icy as Uncle Sebastian's gaze. Behind them both is a large stone fireplace. There isn't a fire going, so the room stays cold. A chill runs up my spine. The only light comes from the cool-toned bulbs hanging from the ceiling. Against each wall on either side of us are giant built-in bookcases. The top shelves are a sharp glass and the cabinet doors hide the shelves below them.

At my silence, Buck steps forward.

"I did it. You weren't paying attention and—"

Uncle Sebastian holds up his hand and Buck snaps his mouth shut. Sebastian points at me, and I look to the ground.

"Yes," I say. "Dad wanted us to ask you for a favor. I doubted you'd give them willingly, so when we started talking about Mom...I distracted you and Buck took three vials from Dad's desk."

I glance up. Uncle Sebastian's lips are pressed firmly together, his eyes turned into slits.

"Idiot..." he mutters under his breath. Then, he meets my gaze. "Why?"

I clench my teeth and look away. I can't tell him about Lorrie. He'd made it very clear back at Huson Labs that he didn't—*and probably never would*—believe time travel could really work... The question is, did I have a better excuse to give?

"I..." I scratch the back of my leg with my foot and glance up at Buck.

"Don't look at him." Uncle Seb crosses his arms. "Just answer the question. Why did you steal the tachyons from my office?"

"I needed them," I snap. "I'd...I'd destroyed my dad's machine by testing it on my own, and used up the last of his reserves. If he couldn't get any more, his life's work would be ruined because of me, okay? I'm sorry."

"You're sorry?" Sebastian raises a thin eyebrow. "You destroy your father's life's work, steal volatile, *dangerous* equipment for a top secret, government-funded project, and the best you can say is a snotty '*sorry*'?"

"Hey," Buck says, standing taller. "She's owning up to her mistakes—"

"No, she's not!" Sebastian grimaces. "She's hiding something—you both are... I can't be part of that any longer. Lorraine, your father practically destroyed himself working on this machine. It *killed* his *wife*—destroyed his *career*... I can't let it take me down, too."

"What are you talking about?" I ask. The hair on the back of my neck rises. I glance at his phone on top of his desk... It'd been going off like crazy last night, but now it sits silent. I look up at him. "What did you do?"

Buck takes a step back.

"Huson Laboratory is sending an associate to question me... I managed to push our meeting to this afternoon, but my job is on the line, Lorraine." Uncle Sebastian has the decency to look guilty as he adds, "I'm going to tell them the truth—everything that I know. They're looking into your father's whole life— friends, family... If you comply with them, maybe they'll be able to work something out. It's your only chance."

"Comply for what gain?" I snap. "They'll take apart the Machine!"

"The Machine?" Sebastian scoffs. "Lorraine, I got a call from Mrs. Huson *herself* last night! She said that the United States Department of Defense is threatening to pull back from *every contract* we have with them if we don't get this situation under control, and once they pull back, they'll silence anybody who could threaten the security of those contracts. If you don't turn yourselves in, it'll get messy. Trust me, I know."

Buck shakes his head. "I...I can't. If my family—"

"Trust me, Buck, your family already knows... Listen, I can't risk my job for you, Lorraine. I can't."

I clench my fists.

"You can't stay here," Uncle Sebastian looks away. "I suggest you turn yourselves in, but...it's up to you. I'm sorry."

"You're sorry?" I mimic his voice with all the angry, vicious mockery I can as I add, "the best you can say is a snotty '*sorry*'?"

Uncle Sebastian glares.

"Fine." I snatch Buck's hand into my own and nod. "Tell them everything. See if we care."

"Lorraine," Buck whispers. I turn on my heel and pull him toward the hallway.

"Good luck," Uncle Sebastian scoffs.

"Goodbye," I snap. I navigate through his home until we

reach the front foyer—then stop and look behind me. Uncle Sebastian didn't follow.

I don't know why, but instead of walking toward the front door, I take a door on the right.

"Lorraine—" Buck stops as I tug on his arm. We travel through hallways until we come to a white door. We slip inside and stop.

I've found the garage. It's a large, gray space with dozens of shiny cars parked in a row. I go to a red convertible and tug on the handle. It opens.

I look over at Buck. "Find the keys."

"Where are we going?"

I huff and sit in the passenger seat. I kick my feet out and cross my arms tightly over my chest. "I don't know."

Buck nods. It takes him five minutes to find the keys on a hook on the wall. The car beeps as he clicks the button. He slides into the driver's seat and looks over at me.

"Where am I driving?"

"I don't know!" I snap. "Just drive!"

Twenty-Eight

WE END UP IN A WAFFLE HOUSE off the freeway. We take a booth in the back. I shift against the thin red cushions. My back aches. My eyes hurt. I just want to go home to my room, where nobody expects anything of me.

A TV hangs from the ceiling on the far side of the restaurant. It's got the morning news. My heart sinks as I see a picture of my house. The TV is muted, but the captions display along the bottom of the screen in jagged black lines. They're talking about my dad's career—calling him crazy. The screen changes to an image of Buck and me, the words "wanted" flashing below us. I sink into my seat and close my eyes.

"What can I get ya?" A thin, redheaded waitress approaches our table. I shake my head and push the menu away.

"Nothin' for me," I whisper. She turns to Buck, who sits opposite of me, his legs stretching out under the table, his feet next to me on the bench. He looks up from the menu.

"Water and two eggs, scrambled, ma'am."

The waitress walks off. Buck leans back and crosses his arms, staring at me. I look at the TV, relieved to find the news anchor has moved on to a different story.

"You know, I don't think I'm going to make it to that interview," Buck finally says. I blink, unsure of what he's talking about for a second. Then it crashes into me like a semitruck.

His interview—the one at the tech company. I close my eyes and sigh. Then I smooth my hair out of my face and collapse forward onto the sticky table. "Oh, Buck—I don't know what to do anymore."

"Obviously," Buck mutters. I sit up with a glare.

"Oh, okay then, what should we do, Buck? I have yet to see you come up with a single idea that can—"

"It's your childhood self that's come to ruin our lives, Lorraine." Buck points at me. He leans forward. "Not mine. *Yours.* I have done nothing but support you, and what thanks do I get? Nothing!"

I glare, my jaw clenched.

Buck shakes his head. "You know, if you had just fixed things with your dad like he wanted, we wouldn't be in this mess."

I slam my hand down on the table—our forks clatter. The waitress glances up from another table and shakes her head. I close my eyes and take a deep breath.

"Alright, okay, I'm *sorry*. Is that what you want to hear?" I ask.

Buck scoffs, then shakes his head. "Sebastian's right...you're not sorry. If you were sorry, you'd be figuring out how we clear your dad's name, or how we turn ourselves in, or—"

"We can't save my mom if we do any of those things, Buck—don't you get it? We're completely and totally screwed, and it's all—"

I cut myself off as the waitress sets down a plate of eggs and two waters. I flash her a pained smile. She grimaces and then saunters away. I rub my temples and groan. *This truly is a total disaster.* Whenever I think things can't get worse, the universe proves me wrong. There's no way I can save my mom now—not with Dad being who knows where and our house locked down in a police investigation.

I stare at the eggs as Buck stabs them with his fork and shoves a bite into his mouth. I look up at him. I can feel my lip quivering, so I press it together and look down at the table.

"I *am* sorry."

Buck looks up. His shoulders fall, and he sets the fork down and nods. "Yeah...me too..."

I twist the edge of my napkin until it tears, then roll it into a ball between my fingers.

"I don't know what to do either, if...that counts for any-thing." Buck scoots forward and grabs my hand. He rubs his thumb over the top of my knuckles. "But whatever we decide to do, we'll do it together, okay?"

I squeeze his hand and try to smile.

A figure approaches our table. "This seat taken?"

Buck and I look up.

Lorrie is standing there with a grin, her hands on her hips. She's got a black shirt and gray jeans. Her hair is tied back into a tight pony. I blink.

"Oh, great," Buck mutters. Lorrie pushes his arm until he scoots over, and she squeezes into the booth next to him.

"Ooh! Yum!" She grins and immediately starts shoving Buck's eggs into her mouth.

"Hey—wait—she can't just..." he trails off, then scowls.

"Sho—" Lorrie swallows, then wipes her chin with the back of her hand. "Are you ready to get Dad back?"

Buck and I glance at each other. Cautiously, I scoot forward.

"But, Lorrie...I thought you didn't want Dad's help."

Lorrie's eyes flick up briefly from the eggs. She shrugs and stuffs another bite into her mouth. "I don't. But at this point, he's all we have left. Besides, I saw the future. Turns out we need him."

"Last time you said that—" Buck snaps his mouth shut as Lorrie holds up her hand.

"That was before," Lorrie snaps, then stuffs the last bite of eggs into her mouth. She turns around in her seat, waving wildly for the waitress.

Buck grabs her arms and pulls her back down. "What are you—"

"Hi! I'd like a Kids Smiley Pancake, three sausages, two hash-browns, and—"

"*Sausages*!" Buck cuts in. "She just wants *sausages*—and two more scrambled eggs. We'll see if you're still hungry after that."

Lorrie scowls as the waitress walks away with the order.

"Let me get this straight," I say. "Before, it *wasn't* a good idea to tell Dad you existed, but...now suddenly it is?"

Lorrie nods. "Yep!"

"What changed?"

Lorrie shifts and looks down at the empty plate. She taps her fork against the side as she speaks. "Not much—well, nothing super significant, at least. I just...realized that maybe he could... provide more than one use. You were right, Lorraine, we need him, which means I was right, since you're me, so I'm really glad we're all on the same page now."

Buck shakes his head. "How are we supposed to find your dad and help him?"

Lorrie grins. "I think it's time I visit good ol' Uncle Seb, don't you? He is still alive, right?"

I look away. "Lorrie, about him... He... We were just at his house and, well..."

"He kicked us out," Buck finished. "His job is on the line because of what we did, and we don't want to put more pressure on him. Besides, he said he wouldn't lie for us."

Lorrie taps a finger to her chin. "Does he know about me, though?"

"No." I shake my head and shift in the hard booth. "You didn't want Dad to know, so I assumed..."

The smell of sausage and pancakes is suffocatingly sweet in here. The door at the front jingles—my eyes are pulled—and I freeze.

Two police officers stand at the front. One turns his head to the side, whispers into the radio strapped to his shoulder. The other is scanning the patrons. I duck and kick Buck from under the table. He looks, swears under his breath, and scoots down in his seat.

Lorrie cocks her head to the side. "It doesn't matter if Uncle Seb knows... What are you *doing*?"

"Because of *you*, the police want to talk to us," Buck hisses. Lorrie grimaces. She squirms around in her seat to stare at the officers. I watch as the redheaded waitress walks up to the host stand and the officers start talking to her.

"Buck—we need to go," I whisper. Buck's already got his wallet out and is throwing cash down on the table. Then he pushes Lorrie out of the booth and shuffles out after her. I scramble to follow.

Buck stalks toward the back—walks right through the kitchen doors. Lorrie hesitates, and I run into her back. She looks up at me, aghast.

"We can't go in there—"

"There weren't any signs—just follow him!" I hiss.

I shove her through the door, glance behind me—I can't tell if they saw us slip in the back.

A man in a greasy white apron glances up from the grill as I hold Lorrie's hand and pull her through the kitchen. Buck is already at the back door, holding it open, motioning for us to follow. Behind me, I hear the swinging doors creak open.

I pick up the pace, dragging Lorrie behind me. We run through the open door into the afternoon light. Buck shuts the door behind us as we make a break around the Waffle House to the parking lot.

There's the patrol car—parked right next to the convertible. I gasp and glance at the windows. I can't see the officers. Buck is already running across the parking lot. He jumps into the driver's seat, scrambling for the keys.

Lorrie's gawking, her mouth open. "That's your car?!"

"Just get in!" I snap and yank her arm toward the shiny red vehicle. Lorrie giggles as she slides into the back. The moment I slip into the car, Buck shifts into drive, and we're flying from the parking lot and down the road.

Twenty-Nine

WE HAVE TO STOP FOR GAS before we can get back to Uncle Seb's house. Buck keeps taking back roads—avoiding the freeway and towns. We stop about a mile from a gas station. It's too dangerous to go to the station. We don't know what sort of alerts they have or what information is being used against us. Despite the sunlight outside, I feel like we're trapped in a dark forest, lost in the middle of the night.

Buck volunteers to make the hike and get gas for us. I watch as he walks down the road, up a small hill, and then disappears from sight. I stare at the road. I force myself to breathe. Each time the light glints off the front of a car as it comes over the hill, I freeze. But none of the cars are silver sedans or mysterious black vans.

It's just Lorrie and me now, sitting in the convertible, top closed, pulled over on a little patch of gravel off a back road. I lean back, kick my feet up onto the dash. Lorrie is sprawled on the leather seats behind me, her arms behind her head and eyes closed, like a farmer after a hard day's work. I clear my throat, and I catch her peeking open an eye.

"Hey," I nod.

She nods back. "Hey."

I bite my lip and look away. "You know...last time we saw each other was...a little rough."

I glance in the rearview mirror. All I can see are her feet propped against the headrest. I imagine what Uncle Sebastian would say, if he was here—how he'd complain about our filthy shoes on the leather. I shift, lean my head back.

"Do you want to talk about it?" I ask.

"Talk about what?"

I grimace. "Our fight."

Lorrie sits up. She leans between the seats.

"We can't fight. We're literally the same person."

I sigh and shake my head. This is pointless.

"But..." Lorrie trails off. She leans back in the seat. I turn so I can look at her. Lorrie's arms are crossed over her chest. "If it was a fight, like you say...I'd want to know just one thing."

"What's that?"

"Do you still want to save Mom?"

I nod. "Of course I do."

"Then we don't have a problem." She smiles and slides back down in the seat.

I hear mosquitoes buzzing outside the car. Cicadas buzz from the trees above us. It takes Buck a little less than half an hour to return with the gas. By the time he does, sweat coats his forehead and back. Lorrie scrunches her nose when she sees him.

"Not a word, Lorrie," I warn, and she holds up her hands and lies back down. Buck starts to fill the tank.

Lorrie suddenly leans forward again, her lips tickling my ear as she whispers, "Just be sure to remember your answer. M'kay?"

I swallow, and Buck slips into the driver's seat. Lorrie leans back and kicks her feet up on the back of my chair. Buck takes a second to blast the air conditioner. I watch as his eyes flutter closed, his hair blowing in the wind. I slip my hand into his and squeeze it.

I should tell him how grateful I am—thank him for how much he's sacrificed for me. How much he's put up with.

I lean forward and press a kiss against the side of his face. I taste salt. He leans into the touch.

"Enough of that," Lorrie gags. I lean away as Buck turns in his seat to shoot her a glare. Lorrie either doesn't notice or

chooses to ignore Buck's steely look. She claps her hands together and bounces in her seat.

"Let's go!" she cheers. "I can't wait to surprise Uncle Seb—
he's going to be so shocked to see me, dontcha think?"

Thirty

BUCK PULLS UP TO THE GATE. He breaks, then glances at me. "Uh…now what?"

I frown, pull out my phone, and call Uncle Sebastian.

He answers on the first ring.

"You *stole* my car!" he shouts. I pull the phone away from my ear. Even though the phone isn't on speaker, I can still hear him ranting. "Not just my car—my *convertible*! You stole my favorite convertible, you sneaky little—"

"Uncle Seb!" Lorrie cries—and suddenly she's snatched my phone from my hands. "Uncle Seb! Uncle Seb! It's me—it's Lorrie! Let us in through the gate!"

The phone falls silent. I can't hear what he says, but Lorrie's eyes widen and she pulls the phone away from her ear.

"He hung up on me!" she gasps. I reach back and snatch my phone, looking down at the cracked screen. *He did hang up on her.*

"Babe." Buck taps my shoulder. I look up. The gate swings open. I pocket the phone as Buck eases the convertible up the drive.

Behind me, Lorrie is practically vibrating in her seat. "How different do you think it is—does he have the pool yet? He promised me he'd get a pool."

She's rambling, her eyes soaking up every detail.

"When were you last at Sebastian's place?" Buck asks.

Lorrie shrugs. "Uh, two days ago—well, two days ago *my* time. Dad gets stressed so sometimes I get to visit Uncle Seb for a while."

I frown, trying to rack my brain and remember when that had happened. I turn around in my seat to look at her. "Lorrie, how long has it been since…the accident, for you?"

She shrugs and squirms in her seat, trying to see past me through the windshield. "Dunno," she says. "Couple months. Why?"

"How long had it been when you and I first met?" I ask. Lorrie shifts. She kicks her feet up and down. It's almost like I can see it—the protective shield that rises in her eyes. Like a glass window suddenly separates us.

"Uhhh…" She tugs on her seatbelt as Buck eases on the brakes. I turn back around in my seat. We're under the large black archway. Uncle Sebastian's already outside. His face is like a storm cloud, angry lightning flashing across the top, threatening to unleash a torrent of rain on all those below.

Before I can stop her, Lorrie is slipping off her seat belt. She scrambles over the top of my seat. I wince as her foot pinches my hand—and then she's out the door, running up the marble steps.

"This should be fun," Buck whispers. We both step out of the car. Lorrie throws her arms wide, then tackles Uncle Sebastian in a tight embrace.

I straighten my shoulders, hold my head high, and walk up the marble steps—only to falter when I see Uncle Seb's expression.

Tears prick the corners of his eyes. His jaw is slack and his arms stick out at his side awkwardly. Lorrie continues to hug him, burying her face in his thick wool sweater. He looks up at me as I approach, his eyes wide.

"What have you done?" he whispers. I cross my arms and look away. This isn't my fault, but of course, he refuses to see that. To hear me out.

"Uncle Seb—isn't this wild? I did it—I actually did it!" Lorrie pulls back, her face stretched into a grin. Uncle Sebastian quickly controls his expression, the horror I'd seen in his eyes vanishing just like that.

"I'm...really not sure what to say." He laughs and scratches the back of his neck. "You're...a paradox."

"Heck yeah, I am!" she cheers, both fists in the air. Uncle

Sebastian puts his hand on the top of her head, and his eyes dart to the tree line. He squints, then pulls Lorrie closer.

"Come inside," he says. He looks up at me. "Both of you."

Lorrie dashes into the house. I move to follow her, only for Uncle Sebastian to grab my arm and lean forward.

"Lorraine," he hisses, "how is she here?"

I yank my arm out of his grip, my teeth clenched. "I don't know. Honestly, I don't. She appeared last week."

Uncle Sebastian looks pale—well, paler than usual. He pushes his long, black hair out of his face. He closes his eyes. "This is a disaster."

I scoff. "You're telling me…"

I stalk into the house. Lorrie is darting around the foyer, pointing at paintings on the wall and squealing at things that are familiar to her.

"New carpet. Cool!" she crows as she dodges up the spiral staircase, two steps at a time. Uncle Sebastian crosses his arms as he and Buck walk inside.

"Lorraine," Uncle Sebastian calls—and Lorrie hurries back down the stairs. Once she reaches the bottom, she crosses her arms and huffs.

"It's *Lorrie*," she mutters.

"My study. Now." Uncle Sebastian turns on his heel and leads us back through the house to his study. I watch Lorrie as she skips after him, her eyes wide and shining. She's got hope in her eyes. I glance at myself in a large, silver mirror that we pass. I've got bags under my eyes. They're dull and brown and full of regret. I shake my head and keep following. I glance back at Buck. He's got his hands in his hoodie pocket as he follows. His hair is ruffled and he's got deep lines etched onto his stony expression. I look away.

"Woah, new couch!" Lorrie grins as we walk into the study. She races over to it, jumps, and flops dramatically against the cushions.

"From the beginning." Uncle Sebastian sits behind his desk. He presses his fingers together and holds his hands just under his chin. "What happened—the *truth*, this time, Lorraine."

I shuffle until I'm in front of the desk. I glance back at Buck, who has already taken a seat on the couch.

"Whoa—look at this!" Lorrie zooms from the couch to the bookcases. She stands on her tiptoes and snatches a glass trophy off its stand. Uncle Seb doesn't move from behind his desk, eyes dark and turned into slits.

"Did you win this?" Lorrie asks. She stops, eyes widening. I can tell by the look on her face that—now that she's stopped talking and bouncing around for a second—she feels the tension in the room. You'd have to use an electric saw to cut through it. Lorrie shifts and sets the trophy back on the shelf. "Sorry."

"This—" Uncle Seb pulls his access card out of his pocket. "*This* is on the line here. My job—everything about my life. Now you owe it to me to give me a proper explanation! I'll ask you one more time." He sets his keycard on his desk and leans back. "What happened?"

I roll my eyes. "It's all Dad's fault, okay? He wanted to test his stupid Machine on something, so we grabbed a box of my old junk and sent it through."

"What was in the box?" Sebastian asks.

"I don't know—junk! Old artwork, a flash drive with my old video diaries on it, a couple of Post-it notes—"

"Your what?" Uncle Seb raises an eyebrow. "What was on the flash drive?"

"My video diaries," I mutter. "Videos where I talk to the camera about my day, or...or what I'm feeling. I never shared them with anyone until—"

"Until you sent it to me!" Lorrie jumps in. She comes to stand beside me and pats my arm. "I got it the night Mom and Dad tested the Machine."

Uncle Seb leans forward. "You used your dad's Machine to send your past self *videos* explaining the future?"

"*No*... I-I mean...not intentionally." I look down at Lorrie and sigh. I drag a hand over my face. "I thought the TIME

Machine would incinerate them—like it does literally everything else…but…that night, Lorrie appeared in my room and she…"

I can tell, even before I say it. I'm going to regret this.

"She said we could save Mom."

Uncle Sebastian pushes himself away from the desk and swears. Beside me, I hear Lorrie gasp, her hands covering her innocent ears. Sebastian puts his face in his hands. Then he looks up. I swear his eyes are dark like the barrel of a gun, pointed at my face. "What were you *thinking*? Going back in time to change the course of history is impossible!"

"Says who?" Lorrie scoffs. She walks around the desk and leans against the front. She reaches forward, picks up one of his fountain pens, and spins it around in her hand. Uncle Sebastian sits very still as he watches her.

"Says your *father*, the man who invented the TIME Machine—and apparently, invented *time travel*." As he speaks, his voice rises to a shout. Then he looks at me, shoulders deflating. "You…can't be serious. *Lorraine*, what would happen to you—*to all of us*—if you changed the timeline?!"

I don't say what I want to. I don't talk about how much better off we'd be—*we'd all be*—if Mom had been okay after that test. Instead, I swallow the lump that's in my throat. I shrug and look away. "It wouldn't change the timeline. Lorrie said that it's different than that. She told me it's like traveling through different dimensions."

Uncle Sebastian pinches the bridge of his nose. "Lorraine—she's a child! She doesn't know the science—the ethics—none of it—and apparently neither do you!"

Oh, I know the rules. I just don't agree with them. Dad's obnoxious sentiments are all but drilled into my skull at this point.

Sebastian sighs and shakes his head. The room goes quiet for a moment. Lorrie moves to the corner of the desk and picks up a book. Uncle Sebastian glares at her.

"Alright," he finally whispers. "Alright, so she visits you from the past. What happens next?"

I shrug. "I...she left and I didn't see her for a couple of days. Thought I'd gone crazy like Dad. Then when she reappeared at work, Buck and I took her to his place. We...tried to get me to remember how to time travel."

"Remember? What do you mean?"

I shake my head. "I clearly can't do what Lorrie can. I... You know I don't remember much after Mom... I-I don't know why I just can't. Maybe I'm, like, distancing myself from the past as much as I can, or whatever."

Lorrie leans forward and holds her hand to her mouth. She pretends to whisper to Uncle Seb, "I think it's a performance issue."

I flick her temple and she yelps. Quickly, she steps away to the right side of Uncle Sebastian's desk and rubs her head, glaring at me.

"Did it work?" Uncle Seb asks.

I shake my head. "No. I couldn't remember, so…so we tried to get the Machine up and running. We thought, *maybe*, if I saw the Machine running, I could jog my memory, but…I ended up destroying the Machine in the process."

"That's when we came to the lab and stole the tachyons from you," Buck interjects from the couch. "Sorry about that again."

"I don't blame *you*, Buck," Uncle Sebastian says.

I scowl at the carpeted floors. "After that, I figured we would just get the Machine to *actually* work—I mean, if it sent back the videos, then it could send me back—"

"I told you, Lorraine," Uncle Sebastian snaps. "Your mom died in the Machine long before any time travel could take place—"

"But that's not true," Lorrie speaks up. She's holding another book, looking it over. "Time travel *did* happen that night." She looks up, her eyes dark. "*I* time-traveled that night."

Uncle Sebastian shakes his head. "I'm still trying to figure out how that's even possible."

Lorrie snorts and sets the book down next to Uncle Sebastian's keycard. "It doesn't really matter how, does it? It happened.

I can do it. All we need to do is get Dad and start the Machine up again."

Uncle Sebastian stands. "Tell me how time travel works. When you go back and step on a butterfly, what happens?"

Lorrie scrunches her nose. "You kill a butterfly for no good reason. What kind of question is that?"

"I'm being serious, Lorrie." Uncle Sebastian sighs. "What happens to your future if you change the past? Does the future change forever, creating a paradox where you grow up not needing to go back into the past at all? Can you ever really change anything, or does everything stay the same no matter what you do?"

Lorrie frowns. She steps forward and leans against the desk, facing him. "Uh, I guess it's, like, different than both of those. You change things, and it creates, like, a different world. So it's really fine to change things because it doesn't matter anyway."

"So, you're Lorrie but from a different dimension?"

"Sure," she shrugs.

"So, why are you *here*?"

"To save our mom—duh!" Lorrie rolls her eyes and waves him off before he can protest. "It's fine, Uncle Seb! It's just creating a different timeline, right? *No big deal*. That happens with every decision we make. That means it doesn't matter how many we create."

"So, why do you need Lorraine?"

Lorrie pauses. She looks up at him, then back at me. "What do you mean? She's *me* but older. Of course I need her."

"What about *this* dimension do you need?" Uncle Sebastian presses. Lorrie frowns. His eyes narrow, and he continues, "Why not a different Lorraine who already knows how to time travel? Why *her*?"

"I just *do*, okay."

"You're lying to us." Uncle Sebastian leans down to her level, his eyes piercing. She squirms. "Time travel can't be racing through different dimensions," he continues. "If it were, there would be differences. Little inconsistencies between you and Lorraine…but there *aren't*. You know exactly who we are—you talk to us like we're from *your* timeline. You're *lying* to us…" Sebastian tilts his head—like he's taking a look at a gadget instead of a person. "You've already tried to change the past, haven't you. Let me guess—it didn't work."

Lorrie looks him in the eyes. She bites her lip and tucks her chin close to her neck. My gut drops and I take a step forward. *He's right*—it's all I can think, all I can whisper in growing horror—*he's right*. I feel like the walls are separating from the floor, from each other, like everything around me is stretching and growing farther and farther away from me. My heart thumps in my chest. Everything about my childhood that she's described—everything I can remember, at least—is the same...down to the tiny stuffed tiger, Bean. If we were from different dimensions... there would be differences.

And, like a freight train, it hits me.

I'm an idiot. I'm a naive, stupid, freakin' idiot.

"Oh my gosh..." the words blow out of my lips like air out of a tire. "*You are...* Why? Why would you lie to me?"

"It's not—but I didn't cause a paradox!" Lorrie whines. "I touched her immediately when I first traveled—if we were the same, we would've imploded or something, right? Besides"—she points an accusing finger at me—"*she* doesn't remember *anything*! Nothing I do here hurts her, *so it's fine!*"

Uncle Sebastian presses his lips into a firm line. "No, Lorrie... you know that's not how it works. The first rule of time travel—you can't play God—"

"I can!" The shout echoes through the room. I hold my breath. Lorrie's cheeks burn red, her fists shake at her side. "I can play God because I *am* a god!" She laughs at this and motions around her. "I can change anything I want—do anything I want! I can travel through time on my command, and nobody—*nobody*—can stop me! I'm *going* to do whatever it takes to save Mom—I'm *going* to make Lorraine remember."

The room is spinning now. I stumble backwards.

"Lorrie—what are you planning to do?" Buck steps forward. She turns around to sneer at him.

"I remember that night—the night I gained the ability to time travel." Lorrie's breaths come in ragged gasps. "Mom was in the Machine, Dad was at the computer. I got all woozy and I fell, and then I woke up in my room and my mom was gone." Tears slide down her round, freckled cheeks. They collect at her chin, then leap to their death, where they vanish into the carpeted floor as if they were never there. She wipes her face with the back of her hand. "So I snuck down to the basement, and then I prayed—I prayed and I prayed, and then suddenly, there was a box. I took the box and I plugged the USB into my computer, and I watched all the videos. I saw my future and I *knew* I could save Mom, so I thought about that moment and I went back, but...but Mom wouldn't get out of the Machine—she—*she refused to listen to me*—but she'd listen to me if she could see—see what I become without her—*see that I need her*!"

Lorrie's sins tumble from her mouth like someone's got a gun to her temple—like she's begging for her life with her hurried confessions.

"So I got ready—I grabbed my purse, and I grabbed Bean to prove to her who I was, and I thought of the future—I thought of that person, and I got to our room in the future, and I convinced Lorraine to help... I know I can only time travel because—because *Mom*—"

Her face scrunches, and a sob escapes her lips.

"Lorraine needs to time travel because she's the only one who can convince Mom to get out of the Machine—she can convince her to stop going in the Machine in the first place!" Lorrie sucks in a breath. Her cheeks are red and splotchy. "I'm only able to do what I can do because Mom died—I can only time travel because she died *in* the Machine...and if someone has to die in the Machine to make someone else able to time travel, then shouldn't it be Dad who sacrifices himself? *It's all his fault anyway!*"

My stomach drops, and suddenly I can see it—a memory flashes before my mind... Lorrie had pushed him—before the Machine had stopped, when the test was just about to work—she'd appeared and pushed him toward the Machine. The only reason he's alive is because he tripped. The countless wires and tubes spread out around the floor had caught him before he could get too close.

I drop to my knees. I'm going to puke. My stomach twists, and I slap both hands over my mouth. I can't breathe—*I can't breathe.* I'm barely aware of Buck's legs as he stands in front of me.

"You can't do that!" Buck shouts. "Lorrie, that's your *dad*—"

"He killed her!" she shrieks. She slams her foot into the ground, over and over and over again. I can see my dad's face beneath her heel—she's stomping out his light, her foot connecting with his nose, blood gurgling from his nostrils, his teeth knocked in. Lorrie keeps shouting, "He deserves everything that's coming to him and more! He should be grateful! I'm going to make Lorraine time travel—with or without your help!"

And then she lunges. She snatches Uncle Sebastian's access card right off the desk and darts away. He makes a mad grab for her, his fingers just brushing the tips of her hair—and then she vanishes in a burst of blue electric light.

Thirty-One

UNCLE SEBASTIAN STUMBLES BACK A STEP. "She...can't be serious," he whispers. He looks over at me, his eyes wide, lips trembling. Guilt twists like a knife in my back. He pierces me with his tormented gaze. "Lorraine, tell me she isn't serious."

"I-I—" I choke on my words and shake my head. My mind is a pinwheel, spinning round and round, getting nowhere. The truth? I can't answer his question because I honestly don't know. I can't remember. No matter how hard I try or think, nothing from my past comes up—nothing between the accident and...and when I started to record those videos.

"We can't stay here." Buck rubs my back. "The lab can track Lorrie when she travels. They'll see the readings. They'll know she was here."

"They can what?!" Uncle Sebastian's shouting again. "And you brought her here?"

"Where else were we supposed to go?" Buck shouts back.

"Not bring her here—turn yourselves in—not play with time travel, like I said in the first place!"

I recognize Buck shouting again, but I can't make out his words. Their voices rise in tone and volume, and I cover my ears and press my forehead to the ground.

I am trying to kill my Dad. Why can't I remember that? Do I succeed? How do I get her to stop? A chill goes down my spine and settles deep in my intestines... *Did I want to stop her?* I shake my head. I want to hurl. A gag forces itself up out of my throat. My thoughts race against my beating heart, faster and faster, until something holds me and squeezes.

Buck holds me close to his chest, my ear against his bicep. I close my eyes and try to breathe slow and steady—but it's not enough, it's never enough to catch up to my trembling body.

I feel him tap-tap-tap rhythmically on my shoulder. His heartbeat is steady and strong in my ear. I close my eyes and listen to it thump—thump-thump—thump—thump-thump.

"Lorraine," his chest rumbles as he speaks. "We have to go."

I nod—*where will we go?*—push myself up—*what are we going to do?!* Tears stain my cheeks. I hadn't even realized I'd started to cry. The world spins, but I manage to stand on my feet with Buck's help.

Uncle Sebastian races around the room—he's holding a brown duffel bag. He's shoving different things into it—a book from his desk, the trophy from his shelf.

"My job—my life—ruined! Down the drain!" he shouts as he races around. "My keycard—gone! This is a disaster!"

Buck grabs my hand, and he drags me through the manor. I wipe the last of my tears as we hit the tile in the foyer. I give his hand a squeeze, then we race toward the front, together. He throws open the large doors, and we screech to a stop.

"Miss Sullivan." Miller is standing on the steps. My breath catches in my throat like I've swallowed a pill that's just a little too big. Miller's grinning like a shark. Three black vans are behind him. There are men wearing body armor—they've got guns. Miller takes off his sunglasses and looks me in the eyes. "What a surprise."

Thirty-Two

I SIT IN THE BACK OF THE VAN with my arms crossed. I can feel the chill of the metal seat under me, and I do everything I can to avoid Uncle Sebastian's even colder stare from across from me. We're the only two in the armored vehicle. They've put Buck in the one trailing behind us—or I assume it's behind us. I can't see anything in this dark coffin. *Is he going to be okay? Why have they separated us?*

The van goes over a bump. The chains around my wrist clank against each other as I grip the seat under me.

"Well, what a lovely afternoon," Uncle Sebastian nods and makes a show of looking around the dark vehicle. I swallow and stare down at my sneakers. He continues, "I always wanted to be kidnapped and shoved into the back of a van. Thank you for the opportunity, Lorraine. You know, while we're at it, we might as well add *murder* to the list—"

"I'm not going to kill my dad." I look up and meet his piercing gaze.

His glare doesn't falter. "But you might just sit back and let Lorrie do it for you, huh? *Newsflash, Lorraine!* That would still be *you* killing your dad."

"Well, I can't change the past, now can I?" I snap. Then, at the irony of my words, I sink back and glower.

"Do you think sacrificing your dad to the Machine will save your mom?" Uncle Sebastian asks, his voice level. "Like it's some sort of god?"

I shift and look up at him. I lick my lips and look away. "What if... What if we just don't do anything? Just decide not to make a choice—"

"Doing nothing *is* a choice," he snaps.

It's a crossroads. My dad or my mom... Who can decide something like that? Who could make a choice like that? If I do nothing, Lorrie will continue on her path...but if I intervene, does that mean I have to leave my mom to her fate? Something shifts inside me. My nostrils flare.

"How painful do you think it was?" I ask.

Uncle Sebastian tilts his head to the side. "What?"

"Dying in the Machine." I look up through my hair at him, glowering. "How painful do you think it was for Mom?"

I watch as his eyes widen—then he presses his lips into a thin line. "That's not fair."

"What if we could do it?" I whisper. "Then come back and stop Dad from dying too?"

"That's a paradox, Lorraine!" Uncle Sebastian hisses as he leans forward. The handcuffs around his wrists catch where they're chained to the seat below him. Still, I scoot away, my back digging into the metal side of the van. Uncle Sebastian sneers. "Don't you see? There's no winning here. You got us sucked into an impossible-to-win situation! It's a loss on all sides—yours, mine, the lab—everyone loses!"

I close my eyes and try to rest my head against the wall of the truck. We continue to rumble down the road—I assume it's a road. We shift from side to side. I can hear the sound of the engine roaring like Buck's truck. My heart aches.

"Where do you think they're taking us?" I whisper. It's Uncle Seb's turn to sigh. He leans back and looks up at the ceiling. Light shines from a tiny square window behind me. It lights up a portion of his face, accentuating the dark purple circles under his eyes. Those soulless, glassy, brown orbs.

"I don't know," he finally whispers. His eyes flick toward me and he scowls—hard and cold. "But you better pray that they don't hurt you."

Thirty-Three

WE SCREECH TO A HALT. I stumble forward. Uncle Sebastian sticks out his twiglike legs to brace himself. Before I know what's happening, someone herds me out of the vehicle and into a big gray building—I catch a flash of the sign: Huson Laboratory. Buck screams my name from behind me—I try to look, but a big, meaty hand forces my head to face forward.

The two men on either side of me drag me into a long, sterile, white hallway. They hold me by each arm. I'm sure there are bruises forming underneath their fingers, which dig painfully into my arm.

They pull me into an elevator. The guard pushes the button for the bottom floor, and we descend. It takes seconds. My stomach jolts as we stop—then the doors slide open and I'm dragged out.

They lead me through a door with a large potted plant next to it. The room we enter is dark. I squint my eyes to try to see, but all I can make out are dark figures and shapes, and I'm led quickly past them and to another door. We step through and finally stop—this room is blindingly bright. I try to blink to adjust my eyes to the light—black shadows are dancing in my vision, dancing on the walls, dancing on my grave. The room is tiled with small white squares on the floor and walls. There's a large mirror built into the wall to my left—*is it one-way? Are they behind it, watching my every move, watching my every breath?* In the middle are two chairs and a metal table. The floor is white except for the silver drain in the very center. I swallow. There's a rusty brown stain next to it.

"Where are we?" I ask as the men drag me further into the room. I yelp as they shove me into the chair, making sure I'm facing the mirror. One grabs my hands and undoes my cuffs, then they both turn and leave.

Silence floods the room, rushing in around my ankles. It rises to my knees, soaks my stomach. It crushes around my neck, and then I vanish in the suffocating emptiness around me. I can't hear anything other than my own heartbeat in my ears. It feels thick in the air, like someone has tossed a weighted blanket over my entire body.

Lorrie is out there—doing who knows *what*, who knows *when*—and I'm stuck in a secret underground prison with no way to contact anyone, let alone anyone who would *actually* care.

I turn to look at my reflection in the mirror and bite my lip. *Is this the face of a killer?* My dark, straight hair hangs around my round, freckled cheeks. Dark circles brood under my eyes. I have dirt smudged on my clothes, I look like I haven't showered in weeks, and my eyes are red and puffy. *I look terrible.*

Part of me doesn't want to believe it—even though I technically confirmed it myself. *I can't hurt Dad...but...if it means saving Mom?* I tear my gaze away from my reflection. *This is a disaster. It's hopeless. I'll rot down here forever.*

And then the door opens, and people shuffle back into the room. I jump to my feet and come face to face with the one person I'd honestly started to believe I'd never see again.

Dad.

He stands across from me, in between the same two men who had dragged me down here. They push him toward me, then leave. The door slams shut behind them, making me jolt. The lock slides into place, sealing me in this tomb. I swallow and look at the shiny metal table.

Dad takes a step into the room—I take a step back. He's got a cut on his cheek. His clothes are rumpled, like he's slept in them. He blinks, takes another step toward me, then another, and then he wraps me in a hug.

I'm going to puke.

"Lorraine," he whispers as he holds the back of my head in his hands. I resist the urge to rest my chin on his shoulder. He squeezes me tighter. "I'm so glad you're safe."

My eyes hurt with sudden pressure, and I push against his chest. His arms fall at his side as I take a step away.

"How...are you?" He licks his split lip, eyes glistening. "Are you okay? Have—have they hurt you?"

Each word is a knife thrust into my heart. I don't deserve the kindness that shines in the tears slipping down his scruffy cheeks. I don't deserve the warmth that's in each hug. I don't deserve the tea he makes every morning or the spaghetti he makes me most nights. My breath hitches. I don't deserve the forgiveness for ruining his Machine—the light of his smile when I come home from work.

I was going to kill him—I was, I *know* I was.

"Lorraine?" he whispers as I collapse into the metal chair. I throw my head into my hands and sobs wrack my body.

He kneels in front of me. Puts his hand lovingly on my knee.

"I'm—sorry!" I choke out the words and wipe at the tears flowing down my cheeks. "Dad, I'm so—so sorry!"

"Shh, Lorraine, there's no reason to apologize." He rubs his thumb on my knee and leans forward, trying to meet my eyes. I roughly turn away from him and cover my face. I don't deserve the look of love in his eyes—the one I've refused to accept, the one I've blatantly ignored. The look I've scoffed at, the look I've mocked when his back was turned.

"No, no, you don't—get it! She... *I-I'm...*"

"Anything, Lorraine." My dad scoots closer to me. "Anything you tell me, and I will still love you... I will always love you."

And just like that, everything Lorrie had told us comes tumbling from my mouth. I tell him how she told me not to tell him—how she'd made me promise. How angry she was when the Machine broke, how she suddenly seemed to change her mind—how I hadn't realized *why* it was suddenly okay to get his help. How I hadn't realized she's planning on using him as a sacrifice, to recreate the events from before. I tell him how desperate I am to save Mom—so desperate I haven't even taken a second to think—*or to care*—about how it will change things, how it will affect him. How I don't deserve his love anymore. I tell him he should be furious with me. *He has the right to be furious with me.*

Finally, after everything spills out, we sit in silence. My dad keeps his hand on my knee.

"Lorraine," he whispers. "I know."

"You know?" I ask through another sob.

He nods. "Yes, I know...I have for a while."

"You...you know what?"

Dad inches forward, and I finally meet his eyes. He's staring at me, gray-speckled eyebrows pulled together, brown eyes staring at me with the intensity of the sun. I swallow thickly and wipe the rest of the tears that keep running down my face.

"I know *everything*," he whispers.

Finally, it clicks.

This entire time—for my entire life—*he knew?* He knew that I hated him—that I tried to kill him, and yet...

The memories come flooding back. He gifted me my first camera—the one I used to record my first video. He kept buying me new art supplies—I'd scoffed at the time. They weren't the brand that I liked. But that didn't stop him from trying. Didn't stop him from getting the new pencils, new markers—even a tablet for Christmas. I thought of the night he encouraged me to go to prom with Buck.

He knew...and yet...he loved me. He loved me through all of that. I blink rapidly.

"How?" I ask. "How could you know?"

"I know because..." He hesitates and glances at the mirror on the wall. He presses his lips together. "I know because you told me years ago. I've known and...and I've been trying to prepare the Machine for you ever since."

I suck in a breath—my mind spins in my head. My entire life is different now—like someone's taken it and tilted it on its edge.

Dad stands and wipes the tears from my cheek with his thumb. Then, he kisses the top of my head.

"Lorraine," he whispers. The door opens. Two men enter—Miller is behind them. I look up to my dad. He smiles. "Whatever is about to happen, know that I love you."

The men grab him by the arms.

"Wait—" I stand as they begin to drag him out of the room. I step forward. "Wait!"

"Remember, Lorraine!" Dad shouts. "Family is everything!"

The door slams shut. My hands shake. I swallow and stare up at Miller. He stares back, his hands clasped behind his back. His face is stony. Even inside, he's wearing the black, soulless sunglasses.

I bare my teeth and glare at him.

"What do you want?" I hiss. "Where are you taking him?"

"I tried to warn you, Lorraine." Miller's voice is soft. He shrugs—picks a piece of lint off the sleeve of his suit and flicks it away. "But you didn't listen to me."

"Listen to what? You threatened me! Threatened my dad!" I step toward him and ball my hands into fists. "I'll ask one last time—where are you taking him?"

"Lorraine…" Miller leans forward. His voice drops to a whisper. "You should be worried about yourself right now."

Thirty-Four

THE DOOR SWINGS OPEN and a blonde-haired woman waltzes through. She's wearing a pinstriped pantsuit and dark, bloodred heels. She's older—in her forties at the least. I can see the lines of time just beginning to mar her face, to wrinkle her brow.

"Thank you, Miller," she acknowledges him as she inspects the cuff of her sleeve. "You can escort Dr. Sullivan to the Backyard, now."

Miller nods, turns, and leaves. The door shuts behind him, and I meet the woman's eyes.

"Hello, Lorraine Sullivan. It's so nice to finally make your acquaintance." She smiles, the corners of her eyes crinkling as she holds out her hand for me to shake. I stare down at it. Her nails are cut short and square, manicured. On each finger is a different golden ring. "I'm Victoria Huson, of Huson Laboratory for Research and Development. Pleased to meet you."

"You've got to be joking," I whisper. Mrs. Huson's eyes flash, and she lets her hand drop. Her smile doesn't waver—doesn't flicker for a second. She moves to the table and sits on the edge, crossing her legs. Her blonde hair falls down her back like a waterfall as she tilts her head to the side. Her pink lips press together into a smirk as I stand in the middle of the room.

"My, my, Miller wasn't kidding. You are hard to read, kid."

I square my shoulders and watch her as her eyes seem to twinkle.

"What are you doing with my dad?" I ask.

She looks down at her nails, the golden rings glint like knives under the buzzing fluorescent lights. She grins.

"Your father is a liability. I don't like liabilities…but that leaves us ladies to have a fun little chat, *hmm*?" She claps her hands together. "Come, sit down, sit down! This will only take a few minutes."

When I don't move toward the metal chair, her grin tightens. "You know, your cooperation has a direct correlation with what happens to Dr. Sullivan."

I click my tongue but stalk forward. I grab the back of the chair, pull it out from the table, and sit, arms crossed. Victoria Huson smiles again.

"Right," she scoots forward. "So, tell me. How do you do it?"

"Do what?" I ask dumbly. She leans toward me, her eyes wide and twinkling with curiosity. Her hair sweeps past her shoulder.

Up close, she looks more like a supermodel than the owner of a morally questionable science lab—what, with her perfect teeth, perfect smile, and green eyes like stolen emeralds.

"Time travel, of course!" she says. "It's been something we at Huson Labs have been trying to do for ages—of course, we've never been able to get anyone willing to work on the project after your mother died. Jessica, was it? *Lovely* woman. Terrible with people, but truly lovely."

I swallow and stay as still as I can. My heart beats rapidly in my chest and I can feel my palms start to sweat. I wish Buck were here. I look away from her intense gaze and try to think of something to say.

"Oh, come on now, don't be shy!" She lightly punches my shoulder, then leans against her hand, her elbow propped up on her knee. "I'm all ears."

"I...I don't know how," I finally whisper. Her face twitches, but her smile never wavers—like a plastic mask, shiny and cheap.

"I said," she whispers, still smiling, "don't be shy."

"I'm not being shy, it's the truth."

Mrs. Huson presses her lips together and her eyes flutter shut. She's got glittery gold eye shadow, her lashes painted in mascara. She inches forward until I find myself pressing back in the chair. I grip the edge of my seat.

"Lorraine Sullivan, you are *cheeky*, aren't you?" She studies my face...then leans back and sighs dramatically. "There's no use lying, kid. We've seen the readings. The radiation that follows you around is off the charts! You can time travel—without a Tocky-on Implementation—*whatever* Machine. You've been doing it since you were just a child. I mean—you told your father just about everything, didn't you?"

I snap my gaze to the mirror on the wall and feel my stomach clench. *Stupid—of course they were listening! They probably had my whole confession on tape.*

I sigh. "Listen, Victoria—"

"Mrs. Huson," she corrects. I falter.

"...Right...Mrs. Huson, I'm being honest. I don't remember how to do it."

"Lorraine—"

"Miss Sullivan," I correct. I watch as her left eye twitches.

"Lorraine," she continues. "You traveled through time and space when you were a child, and you expect me to believe that you just '*don't remember*' how to do it?"

"Yeah, 'cause that's the truth."

"How about this?" She stands. Her bloodred heels click against the tiled floors. She steps over the drain and rests a slender hand on my shoulder. A shiver goes up my spine. "Tell me how you're able to time travel, and I don't kill your father."

My gut drops. I stare ahead, eyes wide.

"Of course, your silence will be bought too—it's only fair," she continues. Her fingers drum against my shoulder. She leans around me to my left. Her breath tickles my ear. "Come now, dear, we don't have all day."

My breath comes in quiet, strangled little gasps as I stare ahead. "I...you wouldn't—I'd go to the police and—"

She laughs—sharp and cold. I flinch away and turn in my seat to look up at her. She grins down at me like I'm a child who's been caught drawing doodles on the wall.

"Lorraine, really... Think about that for a second." She strolls around me and sits down on the table again. "You go to the police, you make those wicked, vile claims...and I have no choice but to sue. I'll take every penny your family has left—well, that *you* have left, because it'll be just you. That'll be hard, won't it? Sure, you could find some lawyers, but you'd need an *army* of lawyers. An army that's better than *my* army of lawyers. We'll take everything from you, and you'll lie awake at night in some crappy apartment you can barely afford, while you work *three* part-time jobs, *and you'll think to yourself, 'Oh gee, if only I'd just been honest with the great Mrs. Huson.* I have only *myself* to blame.' Do you want that, Lorraine?"

Numbly, I shake my head.

She grins. "Good. Now tell me how to time travel."

Desperation tugs at my voice, and I blink away the tears that are stinging my eyes. "I-I can't!"

She groans and lets her head fall back. "Oh, come on, Lorraine! It's simple—it'll be our little secret. I won't tell anyone, I swear."

I lean toward her. "I told you, I can't. I don't remember how—if I did, I would tell you!"

Mrs. Huson clicks her tongue. "Well...that's a shame, Lorraine, a real—"

The lights above flicker out and we're cast into darkness. Then, seconds later, they click back on. Mrs. Huson glares at the ceiling. She shakes her head, as though the flickering bulbs had personally offended her, then turns back to me.

"Well, time's up," she claps her hands together. "That is such a shame. Your father was a brilliant man. Terrible with people, but brilliant nonetheless."

"Please," I whisper. "I would tell you—I would tell you if I knew how, but I—"

She holds up her hand to cut me off. "I'm bored now. You can sit here for a couple of hours and think about telling me or not telling me. It doesn't really matter to me. I have no real stakes in this game, but you…you should think about how much your dad can suffer before his heart gives out."

I watch, an ice-cold hand of horror squeezing my heart as she waves and walks toward the door.

"This has been…well, dreadfully boring and entirely unproductive, but it was really nice to meet you, Lorraine. Toodles!"

She strides through the door and it slams shut behind her. The lock echoes around the room, jeering at me, taunting me with the keys just out of reach. I fall back on the metal chair. Fury burns through my veins, and shame wraps a rope around my neck.

This is all my fault. If I'd never given that stupid box of junk—if I'd never put that stupid video diary in the Machine… I look up.

I can't change the past, but maybe…maybe I can change my future.

I stand, grab the top of the metal chair, and take two quick steps toward the mirror. I hurl the chair up and crack it against my reflection. The chair clatters to the floor. I look at the mirror. Not a single crack.

I roll my shoulders, bend, and pick up the chair again. I hoist it in the air and freeze as the door bangs open from behind me. I whirl around—ready to throw my only weapon—then stop as I recognize the man who's come in.

"Uncle Sebastian?" I shout. He stands halfway in the door, eyes wide, an arm up to cover his face—*probably to protect himself from the chair.* I set it on the ground and step around the table. "What are you doing?"

"Breaking out." Uncle Sebastian holds up a shiny access card and grins. "You didn't think I only had one access card, did you?"

I dust off my jeans and take a step toward him. I hesitate.

"Uncle Seb...a-about..." I look away. "I'm sorry. I-I shouldn't have—"

"This is great and all, but we really need to get going." Uncle Sebastian steals a glance inside the room, then looks back at me, in the eyes. "I know, Lorraine. *I know.* Let's go save your dad."

Thirty-Five

I STAY A STEP BEHIND UNCLE SEBASTIAN. He's lost his hair tie, and his shoulder-length strands bounce against his neck as we run out of the interrogation room. I stumble as we enter the darkened observation room and snag Sebastian's elbow for support. We weave around the darkness until we come to another door and burst into the hallway. I blink, then look at Uncle Sebastian. He's got dirt on the knee of his pants and a fresh bruise forming on his jaw, but he doesn't seem hurt other than that.

I look up and down the white, sterile hall. There aren't any Huson employees or security guards yet—*maybe they haven't realized we're out*...which means we're racing against the clock. The longer they don't know we're out, the better chance we'll have. It'll only be a matter of time before they realize... Only a matter of time before they decide to bring us to the "Backyard," whatever that is. Only a matter of time until there isn't time left, and it won't matter that I decided I can't hurt my dad—because that decision is about to be made for me.

"Where's Buck?" I ask as Sebastian rushes across the hall to another white door. He swipes his access card on the side. The light turns green, and he pokes his head inside.

"That's what we're trying to find out." Sebastian leaves the door open and goes to the next one on his right. I spin around. There are only four white doors in this hall. Behind me is a solid wall, with a large oil painting of Mrs. Huson. She's got a pearl necklace wrapped tight around her throat, her cheeks pinched into a perfect smile.

I *hate* that smile.

At the other end of the hall, there's a bend—that must be where we came from. That's the way out.

Sebastian's moved down the hall—he's checked two more doors. Still no Buck. My hands tremble and my arms shake, and I feel like I'm hooked up to an IV of anxiety. Uncle Sebastian's at the last door, and I stumble after him.

The panic is replaced with a wave of relief. *It's Buck.* He's sitting in a white room—I'm looking through a one-way mirror on the wall. Sebastian's already rushing toward the locked door. I rush up to the mirror. Buck's shoulders hang as he slumps in the chair. His face is buried in his hands. A lump catches in my throat. *What did they say to him? What have they done to him?* Sebastian unlocks the door and throws it open. I push past him, shoving myself inside.

Buck jolts up, his eyes widening.

"Buck—" I'm cut off as he launches across the room and wraps me in his arms. I close my eyes and press my cheek against his jaw. He pulls back, looking me over. I reach up and run my thumb over a cut on his cheek.

"You're alright," he whispers—almost like he can't believe the words he's saying. Then, he smiles. "You're safe."

"Touching—*very touching*—time sensitive task here!" Sebastian snaps from behind us.

I wrap my hand around Buck's arm and pull him toward the door. "He's right—there isn't much time."

Buck follows and squeezes my hand. "Where are we going?"

I squeeze his hand back. "We're going to save my dad."

Buck bursts into a run and begins to drag me behind as he says, "*Finally!*"

Sebastian leads us back into the hallway. We slide around the bend and come to another short hallway. I see the elevator—there's a security guard.

Buck rushes him.

The guard shouts—reaches for his gun on his hip. My heart

leaps into my throat. Buck kicks him in the chest, and the guy stumbles back into the metal door of the elevator. A strangled grunt escapes the guard's mouth as Buck rams a shoulder into his stomach. The guard slides to the ground and, in a flurry of movement, Buck straddles him like you'd straddle a bucking horse. He wrestles the gun out of the guard's hands and tosses it across the room. It clatters against the floor as it slides on the gray, laminate tiles.

Sebastian and I rush up.

"What do we do? *What do we do?!*" I wipe my palms on my jeans as Sebastian reaches down and grabs hold of the man's feet.

"His arms—get his arms!" Sebastian hisses. "We'll lock him in an interrogation room!"

The guard's eyes widen. He opens his mouth and lets out a wheeze—then curls in on his stomach. Buck wraps his arms under the guard's arms, then hoists him up. Sebastian grunts, and I watch as they shuffle back down the hall.

"The door—Lorraine, get the door!" Sebastian shouts, and I jump back into action. I throw open the first door on our left and step out of the way. Uncle Sebastian and Buck carry the security guard through the dark observation room. Seconds later, they come out without the guard.

"Okay, now what—where's your dad?" Buck asks. Sebastian's

holding his access card in his hand, his knuckles white. My legs are trembling. I smooth back my hair as I shake my head.

"I thought he'd be in the interrogation rooms..." Uncle Sebastian raps his knuckles on his forehead. "Think, Sebastian—think!"

"Why does your place of work even *have* interrogation rooms?" Buck mutters.

I tug my hair. "Where's the Backyard? They told me they were taking him to—"

"The Backyard?" His face pales, and he swears under his breath.

"What?" I step toward him. "What's the Backyard?"

His gaze trails the floor. "We...*it's*..."

"What is it?!"

He meets my gaze. "Nothing good." He shakes his head, then squares his shoulders. "Come on—this way."

"Where are we going?" I hurry after him as he stalks away from the elevator and down a small hallway to the right. He presses his access card against the side of another door and steps inside.

"Lock it," he commands as we follow. I nod and lock the door. The room is cold and small. Monitors are crammed into the far wall, hanging from the ceiling and piled on the desk. Dozens of images are displayed on each screen—it seems to be the security feed from around the entire facility. There's a keyboard underneath the dozens of all-seeing eyes. I take a step closer to the screens. Buck's eyes widen.

"Find him—he's here, somewhere," Uncle Sebastian motions to the keyboard as he starts inspecting each monitor for a sign of my dad. Buck descends on the keyboard like a panther on its prey. His fingers fly, and I watch as the monitors flicker. The one in front of us changes to just one image—a white hallway with nobody in it. The screen changes rapidly as Buck clicks through the different feeds.

I point to the figures on the screen. "There! That's Dad!"

Two security guards pull Dad down a hall. Miller follows behind them at a leisurely pace, his hands resting in his pockets. My stomach flops. "Where are they taking him?"

Uncle Sebastian runs a hand through his hair. "The...the Backyard is where we send experiments that need to be..." He looks away from the screen. "*Disposed*."

"Guys!" Buck's voice breaks, and we look back at the monitor. The image flickers, distorts, then turns completely dark. My heart hammers in my throat. Seconds later, the security feed powers back on.

"What was that?" I ask.

Uncle Sebastian shakes his head. "Power outage..." He points to the screen. "Where did George go?"

The three of us scan the security feed. He has to be here—he can't be gone, not yet. I scan each monitor, eyes jumping from screen to screen until I find one that shows a white, sterile room. It's large, packed with dozens of tables. Each one has a different experiment—a different piece of bizarre, inhumane invention. And there, entirely out of place in the middle of the room, looking like a kid who just landed in a field of free ice cream, is Lorrie.

Thirty-Six

I HISS AND PRESS MY FINGER AGAINST THE SCREEN. "*Lorrie!* What is she doing here? What's she grabbing?"

Buck clicks on the feed and it expands on the monitor. Uncle Sebastian leans forward, squinting. Then his mouth drops.

"She can't take that!" He sounds indignant. "She—that's dangerous!"

"What is it?!" I snap my attention back to the monitor. Lorrie's in the hallway—the same hallway as my dad. She's holding something in her hand. I watch, my stomach knotting, as she sneaks down the hall—sneaks toward Miller.

He notices her a second too late. He turns—reaches for something on his belt—and freezes as she slaps something onto the side of his neck. Lorrie scrambles back, pulls a walkie-talkie out of her pocket, and speaks into it.

The security guards stop at the commotion—they turn around.

"Why isn't he doing anything? Why isn't he grabbing her?" I chew on my thumbnail as Miller blinks. He shakes his head. Lorrie holds the walkie-talkie back to her mouth. One security guard leaves my dad's side and walks forward, hand on his hip. He says something to Miller.

"Oh, no," Sebastian whispers. "It *works*."

"What works?" I shout.

That's when Miller attacks.

He lashes out at the security guard—grabs him by the collar, hurls him through the air, and slams him into the ground. The security guard lays motionless. Lorrie jumps up and down. My mouth drops.

The second security guard shouts and pulls something from his belt. Miller takes three quick steps forward and, in one swift move, disarms the second guard and pins him against the wall. He grabs the back of the guard's hair, slams him into the wall once, twice, three times, then lets him drop.

There's a dark stain on the wall. Bile rises in the back of my throat.

"*Sebastian…*" my throat sounds like it has gravel in it. "*What* did she *take?*"

Uncle Sebastian's staring at the screen, his hand covering his mouth, his eyes wide and pupils tiny. His eyebrows are stretched up, scrunching together in the middle of his forehead.

"It's…not supposed to work," he whispers. He scrubs his hand over his face. "It's a coercive persuasion module. It—it was supposed to be developed for cognitive behavioral therapy. The device, once connected, sends specific signals to your prefrontal cortex. It pulses with electricity, making the user more susceptible to suggestion."

"What?!" I snap.

"Mind control!" he shouts back. "It's a mind control device!"

"Why are you producing mind control for the US Government?" Buck yells.

"I don't know anymore!" Sebastian howls. "Besides, it doesn't even work—it's not supposed to work! The side effects, they… Being under someone's suggestion like that can drive a man mad!" He turns away and lets loose a string of curses. He shakes his head—tears himself away from the security feed and toward the door. "We need to go. Now!"

Buck leans forward and rapidly types on the keyboard.

"What are you doing?" I ask. His fingers dance on the keys, like a pianist during a big concerto. I watch as the screens flick off, one by one.

"If we do anything else illegal tonight, I don't want it caught on tape," Buck says. He paints the final strokes across the keyboard, stands, and together we rush out of the security room.

Thirty-Seven

WE'RE IN THE ELEVATOR, flying up toward the surface, when Sebastian jabs his thumb on another button and we slow to a stop.

"What are you doing—we need to get upstairs to Lorrie before—" I stop as the elevator doors slide open and Uncle Sebastian rushes out. "Uncle Seb!" I cry. Buck grabs my hand and pulls me out of the elevator. We hurry to catch up with him as he jogs down the hall.

"Pit stop!" Uncle Seb says, screeching to a halt in front of a door. He swipes his keycard, then slips inside.

It's his office. I stop as I stare at the desks—my mom and dad's space. Uncle Sebastian is digging through his desk, rifling through drawers.

I see the memory device on its stand. I take a step toward it, but then Uncle Sebastian stands, holding up a small, rectangular device with two menacingly sharp antennae at either end.

"Eureka, as the kids say."

"What is that?" I ask. Uncle Sebastian pockets the device and grabs my hand. I spin toward the door, my back to the desks. Buck is behind me.

"This is a pocket EMP," says Uncle Seb. "Temperamental and highly experimental."

I shake my head. "A—what? Why do we need an EMP?"

Uncle Sebastian snatches my wrist in his hand and squeezes.

"Lorraine, look at me." He takes a breath, searches my eyes. "Lorrie told us what she wanted, right before she stole my keycard. She's here for one thing and one thing only...the Machine, and it's too dangerous. We have to destroy it...for good."

I look down at the device in his hands, then nod.

"Okay," I whisper. I turn around to tell Buck it's time to go, but stop as he stuffs both his hands in his hoodie pocket. "What are you doing?" I ask.

Buck shrugs. "Nothing, I just—nothing."

I open my mouth to say something, but then Uncle Sebastian rushes out of the room and I'm forced to run after him.

My sneakers squeak against the aluminum flooring. My heart races in my chest. We rush down the hall toward the elevator, and I screech to a halt. Three security guards are in the elevator, and the doors are just sliding open. One of them points at us—I turn and run in the opposite direction.

I hear footsteps thundering after me, their stomping echoing in the hall.

"Now what?" Buck shouts.

"There's a fire escape on the other end of these halls!" Sebastian huffs. We turn a corner. My lungs burn. I have to run farther, run faster. I can still hear the security guards chasing us. I force myself to suck in a breath—I try not to think about how deep underground we are—try not to let the panic claw at my throat. We round another corner to find another set of double doors at the end.

Uncle Sebastian slows, his eyes wide.

"Keep up, old man!" Buck shouts. He wipes his brow, sweat clinging to his shirt. Uncle Sebastian ducks his head and pushes forward. He pulls at his turtleneck sweater, his cheeks red.

We burst through the double doors, and I stop, my eyes wide.

"No," I whisper. Horror like ice pours over my scalp. It cascades past my forehead, soaking me to the very marrow of my bones. It races down my spine, pooling in my stomach. I slap a hand over my mouth. Uncle Sebastian keeps running.

"Is that…" Buck trails off. We stare at the large contraption in the middle of the room. Even though it's half built—even though the tech is newer, shinier than anything we've ever seen—we can still tell what it is.

It's a TIME Machine.

Thirty-Eight

IT REMINDS ME OF THAT ROOM in Stranger Things—the one where the Russians are sticking their nose into the upside down. The room is split into two levels. I'm standing on a cat-walk-like ledge. Crowding the space around me are computers and machines. I stumble back. The floor beneath my shoes is a narrow metal grate. I see the ground far below me—my vision spins.

I stumble to the railing and grip the metal safety bar. My legs shake. In front of me is a large space, with metal staircases spiraling to the level below us. In front of me, built up onto a platform, dangling in the air like a carrot on a stick, is a half-built TIME Machine. Large tubes dangle from the ceiling like the strands of a spiderweb.

"What are they doing?" I stand, leaning against the railing. My voice echoes in the vast space. "Why would they have this? They stopped experimenting on this when..."

I whirl toward Uncle Sebastian. He shakes his head and keeps moving.

His footsteps echo against the metal grate. "We need to keep moving."

I stalk toward him. "You told me they stopped working on this! You lied!"

Uncle Sebastian whirls around and seizes me by the arms. I gasp and try to take a step back. His grip tightens.

"We don't have the time!" he snarls. "You think I don't understand the implications of this? Of the technology *I* helped create? They lied to us both, Lorraine! We don't have time to sit here and figure out why!"

I snap my mouth shut, eyes wide as he shakes me.

"We have to keep moving!" he hisses. He lets go of me and storms toward the second set of double doors. They swing wildly on their hinges as he marches through.

I turn and look back at the Machine—stumble toward the doors. Buck grabs me by the arm and tugs. I feel sick. Like I swallowed a brick. They have no idea what they're playing with here.

Finally, I turn and rush after Uncle Sebastian, out of the room and down the hall. I glance over my shoulder at the half-built TIME Machine as the doors swing on their hinges. I let out a breath and pump my legs. I duck my head and run. We have to keep moving.

No matter what Huson is up to—no matter if Uncle Sebastian is in on it or not. No matter what, there's one thing that matters right now. One thing that should have mattered to me since the beginning.

Dad.

We slip around another corner and come to the staircase.

It takes longer than it should to climb the rest of the way up—longer than we have. By the time we reach the first floor, we're all gasping for air. I pause at the door and rest my head against the cool, metal surface.

"Wait—" Sebastian reaches forward. He rests his hand on the door handle. He swallows hard. "They know we're out—they'll have put the place on lockdown."

Buck nods and rolls his shoulders.

I recall the metal tubes surrounding the lobby from our tour and close my eyes. It'll be impossible to get through those. Impossible to sneak past any guards and get through those metal sheets—and if we do manage to do that, then what? Like we'll just be able to walk out of here...

I press my palms to my forehead and try to take a breath.

Sebastian pulls out the EMP. "We can't fight them all, but... maybe...maybe we can lie to them."

"What?" I ask—and before I can stop him, Sebastian walks confidently through the doors.

"I've got a bomb and I know how to use it!" he shouts...to an empty room.

I step into the lobby from behind him. There's not a guard in sight—no one rushing toward us, shouting at us to stop. All the lights are on and...it's empty.

The front desk is to our left. The big open windows tower above us. It's clear. We're not on lockdown at all.

"Something isn't right," Sebastian whispers, pocketing the EMP. I feel like something's watching me, the hair on the back of my neck rising. Like I'm a little bird trapped in a cage, and the housecat is just out of sight, licking its maw. I take another step over the white tile, spin around, and look up at the balcony. We're alone...

"Lorrie... This has to be Lorrie, she...did something," I say. I walk toward the front desk and freeze.

That's when I see the first body.

There are five in total—all out cold and piled like corpses behind the front desk. Security guards. I grit my teeth and look away. Miller—it had to have been him. I saw how he handled those two security guards from before... I didn't want to think about how he handled these—what Lorrie had made him do.

No...scratch that.

This is what *I* had made him do.

I clench my fists and rush toward the front doors—they swing open and we step into the parking lot. Buck jogs toward a black van.

It's time to end this.

Thirty-Nine

WE STEAL ANOTHER CAR. I shouldn't feel bad at this point, since apparently it's become a habit of ours, but I still do. Just a little.

It's not a convertible this time, but one of those big black vans. I sit in the back, on a bench. I grip the seat tight as the van rocks, Buck taking a corner too fast. I grip the seat again to keep from flying forward as he presses the brakes. I lean down to sneak a peek through the windshield.

I see my house. Yellow police tape is strung across our front yard, around our entire property. The early rays of sunlight are only an hour or so away. There's one police cruiser still parked outside...right next to a silver sedan.

"Do you think the police are watching the house?" I whisper.

Uncle Sebastian nods. "Most assuredly."

Buck hisses a curse and slides down in his seat. He turns the car's headlights off and pulls over to the curb. I drum my fingers on the back of his seat.

"You know the house better than anyone." Uncle Sebastian turns around. He hands me the EMP. "Buck and I will cause a distraction. You take this and you destroy the Machine."

I nod—I go to leave—his hand catches me.

"You *destroy* it, Lorraine," he insists. "No matter what."

I hesitate for a split second.

I shove the EMP in my pocket and nod. "I got it."

I slip out the side door. There's no time to protest, no time to argue, no time to think about whether I can actually do this or not. All I can do is pray that my dad's still alive.

I crouch low to the ground and creep through the bushes and trees. I hear the van rev to life. I pause and glance behind me as the black van speeds forward and starts doing donuts in the middle of the street. I think I can hear Sebastian screaming from inside the van, but I can't be sure.

The police car's headlights click on—the siren blares on.

Distraction: *Success*. Now all they have to do is get away.

The van does three more circles, then peels down the street, leaving two black tire marks on the asphalt. The police cruiser speeds after, the lights flashing.

I sneak around the trees and come to the backyard fence. I

jog through the gate, careful to latch it behind me, and ease up to the back door. I jiggle the handle—*locked*. I clench my teeth and cast a quick glance around the backyard. It's silent, the only movement the leaves blowing in the wind.

On any other night, I would have considered it peaceful.

I creep to the kitchen window, slide it up, then crawl through.

Forty

I LOWER MY FOOT DOWN onto the kitchen counter, careful not to knock over any dishes. The spirit of a trapeze artist must inhabit me for just a moment, because I somehow manage not to make a sound as I ease myself down from the counter and onto the kitchen floor. I crouch low and duck next to the island, then poke my head into the next room.

Nothing. Empty. Not a single Huson Labs worker, and no sign of Lorrie. While it's still dark inside the house, I can see the mess left by the police. Every bookshelf had been emptied onto the floor. Pillows are thrown off the couch, some ripped straight down the middle, their insides billowing out like the intestines of a decaying deer on the side of the road. The coffee table's tipped over on its side. My eyes shoot to the mantel, and I feel like I've been punched in the stomach.

My mother's pictures are gone. I rush into the family room,

and my sneaker crunches something. I look down. The photos litter the floor. The broken glass from the frames shimmers like a thousand stars in outer space.

Is this what I've done to our family? What I'm *doing* to our family? Trampling and breaking everything within reach?

Why couldn't I have just listened? I sniff—wipe an escaping tear with the back of my hand. My family is broken. It's tattered and torn, and covered in shattered glass and broken dreams like the pictures of Mom discarded on the ground.

It doesn't give Huson Labs the right. It doesn't give them the right to come in here—to stick their noses in something that doesn't belong to them. To trample over everything Dad has tried to preserve.

I scowl. *They'll pay for this. They'll regret everything.*

I turn on my heel and march toward the basement door. I wrap my hand around the cool metal, then suddenly I'm knocked off my feet by a dark figure.

We tumble to the ground as I shriek. I kick, scrambling away. My foot connects with its nose, and I hear a grunt as I manage to wriggle free. I scramble to my feet, reach for the lights, and stop—are there more police cruisers outside? Were they watching the house from somewhere we haven't thought of?

That hesitation is all it needs. The figure—a man—stands and spits on the ground.

"I tried to be nice," he growls.

I squint into the dark. "Miller?" I take a step back, then another, until I'm walking backwards into the living room. "Where's Lorrie?"

"This—this thing—" he hisses, pointing at his neck. I can just barely make out his figure with the help of the streetlamps outside. Miller grunts like he's in pain—his shoulders jerk and he leans heavily to the left. "It's—messing with me! What—what did she do to me?"

A breath catches in my throat. I know what he did to those security guards—the blood crusted on their temples is burned into the back of my eyes. My mouth feels dry.

"Miller—" I cut myself off as he growls. A deep, animalistic rumble in the base of his chest permeates through the entire room. He looks up—I swear I can see his eyes glinting in the dark like a tiger. My heart beats wildly and I take another step back, until I'm up against the window. My hand twitches. *Where is my taser?*

Upstairs—on top of my dresser. That's where I saw it last.

"It hurts," Miller's voice pitches into half a whine, half a sob. He groans and claws at his neck, sucking in gasps. "*It h-hurts!*"

"Y-you're going to be okay," I say. I'm trying to keep my voice calm, but even I can hear it waver. Slowly, I step around the brown leather couch. "Just...let me take it off. I'll take it off, and then you can tell me where Lorrie is and we...we can stop her, together."

I keep myself facing the window as I inch toward the entry-way to find the stairs. Miller coughs—shakes his head.

"She...she told me..." he groans again, clutching his head. "Her voice—it won't stop—make it stop!"

The lights in the room click on all at once. The TV blares in the corner, my dad's CD player lets out a scramble of Spanish opera, shrieking at full volume. I look up at the ceiling, eyes wide as I watch the lights pulse with energy. I look at the basement door. *The Machine is on.*

Miller's eyes widen. In the lights, I finally catch a glimpse of him.

His hair is standing hackled, on end like the neck of a dog ready to attack. His eyes are bloodshot and...hungry. White foam drips from his mouth and clings to his chin like a barnacle on the side of a ship. His suit is torn on the right sleeve.

"She told me to stop anyone—" he cuts himself off with a scream, his eyes squeezing shut. I sidestep around the couch and hesitate. He needs help—I have to fix this! He looks up at me and something in his eyes changes. They glaze over. He sways from side to side.

The lights flicker, then power off and we're cast into darkness. I can hear Miller's labored breathing, and under his breath he growls, "*Stop anyone from reaching the Machine.*"

Miller lunges toward me. A scream rips itself from my throat as I scramble back. I hear his shoes squeak on the wooden floor, feel the tips of his fingers brush my cheek—I turn and run through the entryway. I slide around the corner—dash for the stairs. I take them two at a time, the wood creaking. Behind me, Miller thunders up the stairs. As I reach the top, a hand wraps around my ankle, and I fall. He snarls as he climbs on top of me—he wraps his meaty hands around my shoulders. I scream, loud and as hard as I can.

I hear a door burst open.

"Lorraine!" Uncle Sebastian yells. Miller hesitates…looks behind us, down the stairs. I pull both knees to my chest and kick him as hard as I can. He stumbles back, slips, and tumbles down the stairs. I roll onto my stomach and scramble to my feet. I rush into my bedroom and jump over the clothes, trying not to trip in the dark. I hear a crash and a shout from downstairs.

"Lorraine!"

"I'm coming!" I yell back as I pat the top of the dresser, squinting to find the taser. *Where? Where is it?* Another crash comes from downstairs, followed by a scream of pain. Panic, like a thousand tiny ticks burrowing in my scalp, washes over me. They're in my hair, tickling my ears—I feel them crawl down my throat. I press my palms into my forehead and force myself to breathe. *Get it together. Get it together.*

I keep searching and finally, *finally*, my hand connects with the familiar plastic. I grab the taser, turn, and stop. Miller is standing in the doorway, heaving for breath. The lights flick back on. I click my taser and hold it out. I test the handheld device— hear the crack of electricity as I press the button.

"Stay back!" I hiss. Miller twists his neck and rolls his shoulders—I hear them crack and pop. His shoulders heave up and down as he pants like a wild beast on the hunt. The lights flicker, pulse, then shut off again.

Miller darts forward.

I jump onto the bed—feel Miller's form brush my back as he trips, crashing into a box. He grunts, and before he can react, I push the taser out and press the button.

I miss. By a mere couple of inches. In the brief flash of light, I watch as his figure leaps back. Before he can lunge again, I jump off the foot of my bed and rush out of the room. I slam the door shut behind me—a second later, I hear a thud followed by the wood rattling in the frame.

"Uncle Sebastian!" I yell as I race down the stairs. I turn the corner into the living room. I scan the dark space. *Where is he?* Behind me, I hear Miller barreling down the stairs. I rush through the living room, over the coffee table, and press my back against the mantel. My sneakers crunch over the broken glass of the picture frames as I wait, watching the entryway, holding my breath.

A figure comes at me from my left—I scream and hold up the taser.

"No—it's me—*it's me*!" Sebastian holds up both hands.

"Holy crap—don't do that!" I scream.

Uncle Sebastian puts his hand on my shoulder. "Lorraine—where's the EMP?"

I reach for my pocket—I don't feel it. It's gone. I scan the floor around me. Where had it gone? When had I dropped it?

"I—I don't—" I step around him toward the basement door. The hair on the back of my neck rises as I hear the growl. Seconds later, Miller barrels through the kitchen doorway and his shoulder rams into me—knocks the air out of my lungs. We fall. The taser clatters from my hand.

I shriek as Miller's once again on top of me. His saliva drips in thick clots over me, pooling on my shirt, sliding down my cheek. He lifts me by my shoulders—slams me down on the ground.

My head cracks against the wooden floor. My vision spins. I see stars. I open my mouth to scream—to cry—and I shut my eyes. I'm lifted again. I clench my teeth.

I hear the electric zap—feel Miller's grip tighten. His fingernails dig into my flesh, and I cry out. Miller's jaw clenches. The lights around us burst on, and I watch as his eyes roll into the back of his head. He shakes and trembles as Uncle Sebastian stands to our right. He presses the taser further into Miller's neck, the prongs of metal digging into the flesh. Miller's tongue protrudes from his mouth, swollen and dripping with red. It mixes with the globs of white foam in the corners of his mouth and then, finally, his shoulders slump and his grip loosens. Sebastian steps back.

The lights pulse, then fade. We're cast into the dark yet again. Miller collapses on top of me and I grunt. I push his shoulders, then shimmy out from under him. Sebastian clatters around the room, then a beam of light shines over us. He's found a flashlight.

I scurry away from Miller on my hands and knees, looking at his prone figure. He twitches once, then twice, then stills.

"Are you alright?" Sebastian asks, voice wavering. I nod. The beam of light shines on the floor and I catch sight of a black metal square. Long metal prongs stick out, dripping in blood. I look over at Miller—there's a wound in his neck, blood oozing and trickling onto the floor. He gurgles and covers his neck with a trembling hand.

Uncle Sebastian steps forward, picks up the black metal square with the edge of his sweater, and holds the thing up.

"Mind control module," he says. "It's detached."

I watch as the prongs twitch, twirl, then retract back into the square. The device stills. Uncle Sebastian sucks in a breath, pushes his black hair out of his eyes, and sets the black metal square back on the ground.

"I found it," he holds out the handheld EMP to me. "Take this and go. I'll make sure Miller's okay."

I snatch the device and scramble to my feet. I slam into the basement door. The lights around us flicker on as I fling it open and tear down the stairs.

Forty-One

I STUMBLE DOWN THE BASEMENT STAIRS. I grip the railing, spin around the landing, and freeze.

There—inside the Machine, the metal arms already circling him—is Dad. He's slumped on the floor, eyes closed. I can feel the pulse of the Machine. There's a blue light in the center of it.

"Dad!" I cry and jump from the landing. I rush toward him. A scrap of metal flies in front of my face. I reel back and look to where it came from. Lorrie's standing in the mess of wires and tubes a few feet away—she reaches down, grabs another scrap of metal, and holds it in the air. She's got a wicked grin contorting her features.

"Surprised to see you," she drawls. In her other hand, she holds a walkie-talkie. She presses it to her lips. "Come down here and stop Lorraine—"

"That won't work!" I snap. "He's not listening to you any-more."

Her eyes darken, and she tosses the walkie-talkie to the ground.

"Whatever," she snaps back. "I've already started the Ma-chine, so you can't stop me now."

I clench my hand, my finger ready on the EMP.

Lorrie looks down, her eyes wide. "What is that?"

"Uncle Sebastian made it. It'll destroy the Machine." I stare Lorrie in the eyes. I watch as the gears turn in her head, watch as her eyes flick from the device to Dad. I step toward her. "Lorrie, you have to stop this. If you don't, I will. Let's...talk this out. We can figure out the best way—"

Lorrie snarls and lunges for the device. I yelp and stumble back. I hold the EMP over my head as she jumps and claws up my body. She's like a starved animal that's seeing food for the first time in months, her teeth clenched, eyes squinting into slits. I stumble back—my foot catches a tube and we fall.

"No—stop!" I shout. My knuckles turn white as I grip the device. Lorrie's grimy little fingers pull and scratch at my hands. She straddles my stomach, pulling and yanking as she tries to wrestle the device out of my grasp—but I hold on tight. *I can't let her have it. I won't.* I grit my teeth and yank my body to the left. We tumble until I'm straddling her. I put my hand over her face and push until she screams—until the device is out of her grip. I stumble back.

Lorrie stands, and I scramble up as well. She wipes her chin. Tears are tucked into the corners of her eyes. Her hair is wild, the static in the air teasing the ends up, pulling them away. She sniffs and looks at me, her teeth grinding together.

"Lorrie! Calm down!" I snap. She half yells, half grunts as she bends down and picks up another scrap. She chucks it at me. I duck and it clatters somewhere behind me. She continues to barrage me with scraps from the Machine. I wince as one hits my arm—another, my leg.

"Ow—*ow*! Stop it, just stop!" I shout.

"You lied to me!" she shrieks. I dodge another scrap, only for one to scrape against my cheek. Lorrie's cheeks are red as she continues to shout, "You lied—you lied! You promised we would save her—you wanted to save her!"

The wind starts to pick up. A wave of heat and energy bursts from the Machine, and the lights flicker. I clench the handheld EMP in my hands. "I *do* want to save her! Don't you *think* I haven't thought about that every day since she died!"

Lorrie slaps her hands over her ears. "Shut up! Shut up! She's not dead—she's not!"

"Yes..." it comes out as a whisper. Pressure builds behind

my eyes. My hair whips wildly about as the metal arms pick up speed. I square my shoulders, and say louder, "Yes, she is. She's gone, Lorrie... She's gone."

"No—no, no, no—" Lorrie screws her eyes shut and shakes her head. I let my hands fall to my sides. I take a step toward her.

"Lorrie. Lorrie!" I shout above her screams. "She's gone and it's not *your* fault, or *dad's* fault, or anyone's fault—it was an accident—"

"You don't remember!" she accuses. "You don't know! You don't remember what I've seen."

"I don't need to see!" I howl above the wind. The Machine is flashing with light. The room around us shakes. The metal on top of the Machine glows bright, hot orange. *I have to end this. Now.*

I hold the EMP up. Lorrie snarls. I push the EMP up in the air, expecting her to reach for it—for her to claw her way up my body until the device breaks. Instead, her arms wrap around my middle, her face pressing into my belly.

Then the world around me fills with electricity. It zaps in arches around me, around Lorrie, like I'm standing in the center of a plasma ball. The hair on my arms rises, my body suddenly alive and vibrant, as the world around me twists—like a piece of paper being crumpled—and I'm cast into darkness.

Forty-Two

I STUMBLE AS MY FEET HIT CONCRETE. My stomach flops, and I close my eyes to keep the nauseating feeling down. I'm starving. Like, if I don't eat right now, I might throw up. My insides are writhing, unsatiated and demanding that I drop everything and eat something—*anything*—right now. I force my eyes open. We haven't left the basement. I scan the room. The technology is brighter, cleaner, yet...older. Nearly ten years older. I spin in a circle. The TIME Machine is to my right, the arms still spinning rapidly. But, instead of my dad in the center of the Machine, it's my mom.

It feels like all the air in the room gets sucked out. Everything in me stops and stills as I stare at Mom. Lorrie lets me go and dashes toward her. My dad is on the other side of the Machine, and though I can't get a good look at him, I can tell he's typing madly at the computer. "Jessica, don't move!" my dad barks.

"Just—stay there, I'm turning it off—stay there! You're going to be okay—it's all going to be okay!"

But I can feel the electricity in the room. The Machine is being powered by something other than the wires along the ground. I force myself to breathe—*in through the nose, out through the mouth*—and look back at Mom.

Her back is to me. The metal arms spin faster and faster. *Why doesn't she just jump out?*

"C'mon—it's time!" Lorrie shouts. She takes a step forward, cups her hands around her mouth, and shouts, "Mom!"

And my mom turns. Her eyes widen. I nearly fall to my knees. There she is—young—younger than I somehow remember her being. Probably eight or so years older than me. We're both in our twenties now.

Her dark black hair is pulled back into a bun. Messy strands stick out around her forehead and whip in the wind. Her eyes are honey brown. She's got a small birthmark on her chin, a tiny imperfection she often tried to cover with makeup. It isn't covered today, and I'm so glad.

"What—" my mom looks down at her hands, gasps, and looks back up. "You—you can't be here!"

"No—Mom, we brought an EMP, we can save you!" Lorrie turns to me and beckons me forward. "Press the button—press the button! You wanted to destroy the Machine, so destroy it!" I stumble forward. I could. I could do it. I look down at my hand, the small, black, handheld EMP trembling in my grasp. I don't have to hurt Dad to do it, either. I just have to press the button. I look up and can see it. How the future will play out.

We would stop the Machine. The power would cut out and the arms would stop moving. She'd stumble out of the center, and Lorrie and I would rush forward. We'd all be crying as we collapsed in each other's arms and sank to the floor. She'd kiss Lorrie's forehead and then she'd look at me. She'd see how much I've grown, and she'd smooth my hair out of my face. Then we'd talk for hours into the night as Dad made us all spaghetti. I'd tell her about Buck—how we'd first met, how he loved me so well, how he pushed me to be a better person. Dad would make a joke about us getting married and the three of us would shush him.

It would work—it can work!

I step forward and raise the device.

"No!" my mom barks, and, instinctually, I hesitate and hold my finger over the button.

Mom is dodging from side to side now, like she's trying to catch my gaze past the wildly spinning arms of the Machine. She flutters from opening to opening, thinking she's found a way out only for the metal to zoom just inches past her nose. She rears back, her hair disheveled. She opens her mouth and cries, "Don't do it, Lorraine!"

"We can do it!" Lorrie cries. "We can save you—"

"If you stop the Machine now, you'll kill us all—I'll kill us all!" Mom shouts. She holds up her hand—my stomach drops. It's covered in blood, flecks of shimmering blue liquid dripping from the tips of her fingers.

"I'm going into time!" my mom laughs. She shakes her head and looks down at her hand. "I'm in time! I'm in time!"

"Mom, you're not making sense!" Lorrie sobs. She turns to me, claws for the handheld EMP. "Push the button—just push the button!"

"Lorraine—don't," Mom says. "If you push that button now, the process will stop and all this pent-up energy…it'll burst like an atom bomb. It'll take you, your father, our neighbors—everything!" She shakes her head. "I can feel it. The energy, the light… It's burning inside my veins, coursing up my arm. It's going to reach my heart any second now. My genetic code is changing—I'm part of this machine now, part of time. I… *It's eating me alive!*"

Her eyes get this distant, glassy look, and I realize the centers of her irises are tachyon blue. She smiles, big and wide, tears like falling stars glisten on her cheeks.

"I can see it all—our life. I'm time. *I'm time.* I'm there at your wedding, Lorrie! It's beautiful—he's so handsome. I'm there for it all—for your children and your children's children. *I'm in time—I'm in time!*"

My mind races.

Lorrie sobs next to me. "Mom, you're not making sense—just push the button, push it!"

I look down at the button in my hand, then up to my mom. That distant look stills for just a second as she stares at me.

I don't understand the science behind it—I don't even try. What I do understand is the look in my mom's eyes. The horror that grips my own throat. The realization that I don't need to understand.

I just need to trust her.

I throw Lorrie off me and stalk toward the Machine. I inch closer and closer, the metal arms spinning faster and faster until I can't see them anymore. The wind beats at my hair as I step as close as I can dare.

My mom stills—she stops dodging from side to side and focuses on me. She holds her trembling hands to her chest.

"Oh—you're so—" my mom's breath hitches. "So *old.* We're nearly the same age now, aren't we?"

And I realize there will be a time when I outgrow her. My hair will turn gray, my skin will wrinkle and sag, my hearing will fade. But she will stay this way—young, scared, fiercely passionate, wildly stupid—forever. Forever in this moment, she would exist. She was *in* time.

"You have to destroy it," Mom shouts. "The Machine—I'm part of this machine throughout all of time, and if it's not—if it doesn't—"

"Mom!" my voice cracks. I can't stop the flood of tears from breaking over the dam I've spent the past eight years building. I look at my mom—into her honey brown, glowing blue eyes. I take in her face, the way her hair falls around her shoulders, the birthmark on her chin. The dark circles under her eyes. The blood coating her hands. The blue tachyon liquid seeping into her veins. Her skin starts to glow. She's a shooting star burning away in the atmosphere. I suck in a breath. "Mama, I love you."

My mom tries to smile. She inches a step closer and swallows hard.

"Baby girl, you're so—" her voice cracks, "beautiful. I love you."

I turn and run.

"No!" Lorrie shrieks. I grab her around the middle and tear her away from the Machine. She claws and cries, and hollers until her voice breaks. She sinks her teeth into my arm and I cry.

The wind around us swirls, papers and stray bits of metal

flying in the cyclone. I hold Lorrie around her middle. She bends forward, pushing against me, trying to get away. I watch, and don't try to stop the tears that spill from my eyes, as light overtakes the middle of the Machine and my mom's figure vanishes within.

"No!" Lorrie shrieks. "No—no!"

"It's time to move on!" I cry above the wind. I think of my dad, Miller, and Uncle Sebastian. I picture Buck in his truck, picking me up from work. I think of all the people who have tried to get their hands on this technology, who have hurt me—hurt my family—because of it. I think of all I've done, all I want to change, and all that I refuse to.

And then, it just happens. I wish I can explain how, but I can't. It's instinctual, like taking a breath of air. It's not something I can explain—it would be like explaining breathing to someone who's never had lungs.

But one second we're in the past, and then I think of my present—Lorrie's future—and the world around me crumbles, the edges folding inward until we're in complete darkness.

Then we pop back into existence.

We're standing before the TIME Machine again, but it's not my mom inside—it's my Dad. Lorrie collapses on the ground, sobbing so fast and hard I doubt she can breathe at all. I clench the EMP in my hand. I move before Lorrie can realize what I'm doing. I walk right up to the Machine and look inside.

My mom had stood there. It was just seconds ago for me, even though I know it was really a lifetime ago. But I can still smell the metallic electricity coursing through the air. The blood that dripped from her arm.

I shut my eyes for a second and turn the EMP on. I toss it through the arms to the middle of the Machine, on top of my Dad.

He's stirring, his eyes still shut. His hair is rumpled, clothes wrinkled.

Can Mom see this? Is she really in time? What does it mean to be in time?

Lorrie looks up from the floor—she hiccups and wipes her eyes.

"What—what are you doing?" she asks, her voice thick. The EMP begins to pulse. The lights in the room flicker. The TIME Machine falters in a shriek of grinding metal as the device does its job. Lorrie scrambles to her feet.

"No—no, no, no!" She dashes forward and I catch her around the middle.

"It's the only way!" I shout above the whirring of the electricity fizzling out around us. Lorrie kicks her legs. She screams and shouts and cries and pleads, but I stand firm.

"You did—such a good job trying to protect us," I cry above

the noise. "Of trying to fix this. But it's *my turn* to fix this now, and I'm choosing to move on!"

Buck races down the stairs. He pushes off the wall, jumps from the landing, and tosses something at me.

I catch it in my hands—I look down at the device.

Sebastian's memory enhancer—I gasp. *No, not enhancer. It doesn't work. It's a mind eraser.* My stomach rolls.

I look down at Lorrie.

She's sucking in deep breaths, her eyes unfocused. I smooth the hair out of her face, grab her chin, and tilt her head up.

"You said—" she whispers. Pauses, takes another breath. "You said you hated him—*we hate him.*"

I clench my teeth, press the device against her eyes, and pull the trigger. I hear a zap, and then Lorrie sags in my arms, unconscious.

Buck slides as he runs to me, scooping me into his arms, hugging me tightly. I let the device clatter to the ground. I rest against his bicep, cradling Lorrie in my arms.

"I hope that worked," I say, even though I know it has. *Because this is why I can't remember anything, isn't it?* I look up at the TIME Machine. The pain of my past has controlled me for far too long. It's time to move on. I watch as the EMP gives one final pulse, the electricity zaps, and the world around us is cast into darkness.

Forty-Three

THE EMERGENCY GENERATOR rumbles to life as the emergency lights click on. The Machine stands still, completely powered off. The arms slowly stop spinning. My dad sits up. His mouth opens, his eyes squinting, as he holds up the handheld EMP. It's charred black. One use only. I'd have to thank Uncle Sebastian for it—who knew how long he'd worked on it.

Lorrie is still unconscious, but I can feel her limbs trembling. I brush a strand of hair out of her face. Her eyes are closed, lips parted. She's breathing, though. I suck in a breath and look up at Buck. He wraps his arms tighter around me, ducks his chin against my shoulder. I feel the pressure build behind my eyes and lean into his touch.

"When did you—" I begin. He hugs me tighter.

"Saw the mind eraser in Sebastian's office, so...I grabbed it. Figured it might come in handy...besides," he sighs, "you... She isn't… You're more than the things she was sayin', the things she was doin'… You aren't her anymore, memories or not, so…" Buck shifts.

"Thank you," I whisper.

"So…now what?"

I look down at Lorrie's head in my lap and lightly trace a circle on her forehead—the way Mom used to when I had a hard time falling asleep. I look into Buck's eyes.

"I have one more thing I need to do."

———————————

I gently set Lorrie down in her bed—the room around me so similar to my own, yet so different. Young—or is it old? Who knows anymore. I find my eyes traveling to the tiny differences. There are fewer clothes on the floor, more stuffed animals along the ground, more art on the walls.

But eventually this room would shape into the room I recognize—my room—and the girl on the bed would be the woman standing over her.

Sitting on the bedside table is the camera I used to record my first video. I shake my head, tempted to take it. Tempted to try and fix it. Instead, I tuck Lorrie into bed, under the covers, and step back. I circle the room, taking it all in for one last time. I catch sight of a box on the floor to my right. I stop.

It's the junk from before—the junk that started this whole mess. Lorrie's laptop is open next to it, the purple flash drive sticking out of the port. I walk over and double-click the mouse. The screen comes alive and I see myself, frozen. The video is paused.

I crouch low to the ground...then press my lips together and press the spacebar.

"I hate him," the young teen on the screen hisses. Her eyes are red-rimmed. Her hair is matted around her face. She's got to be fourteen, fifteen at the oldest.

I remember recording the video. The anger that seethed through my bones. Teen Lorraine begins again. "He—he killed her and he's not—he's not even sorry! If he hadn't run that stupid machine, if he'd just—just—*agh*! I wish he'd just disappear. I wish he was dea—"

I pause the video and close my eyes. Then I unplug the drive and drop it in the cardboard box. I search through her laptop to make sure Lorrie hasn't downloaded any of the videos.

I can't fix the past. I know that now. But, just like a nature walk, I can make sure that I'm leaving things the way they should be.

I grab the box of junk and stand.

The door behind me creaks and I freeze.

"You have five seconds to get away from my daughter."

I turn around. My dad leans against the doorframe, his arms crossed, his eyes narrowed. I suck in a breath.

"Hey, Dad."

He straightens. "Excuse me?"

I shoot a glance over my shoulder at the sleeping Lorrie and hold a finger to my lips. Then, I walk into the light, toward Dad. I watch as his face pales, his eyes widen. He stumbles backwards. I ease the door shut behind me.

"You're—*Lorrie*?" He presses his palm against his forehead. "No, no—you can't be here—you—what are you doing here? I-if you're...then the Machine works and—your Mom—we can go back and—"

"No, we can't," I whisper. "*We can't play God.*"

Now that I'm out in the hall, I can see him properly. He looks so young compared to the man I know. His skin is softer, less wrinkled. His hair is a more vibrant shade of brown. I swallow. There's so much I want to tell him—to warn him, confide in him, comfort him...but I have a mission. I look behind me, at the door to my childhood.

"You know that she loves you, right?" I ask. I swipe away the tear that slips from my eyes. "She just... She doesn't know it yet. You...you have to remember that she loves you, okay?"

My dad looks at me, then takes a step toward me. He gently cups his hand against my cheek. "You look tired."

I laugh and wipe away the rest of the tears. "So do you. Come on. We need to talk."

I head down the stairs toward the kitchen.

"Wait—where are you going?" He follows after me.

"To find some food—I'm starving. You got any pasta?"

Forty-Four

I TELL HIM EVERYTHING over a microwaved bowl of leftover spaghetti. It's got Mom's special tomato sauce, and the taste of it brings a new wave of tears to my eyes. I manage to choke past them as I tell him about how Lorrie had come to visit me, how she'd lied to me about time travel, about Miller—all of it. Then, I finally tell him about what Lorrie does to him. How she tries to trade his life for Mom's. I can't meet his eyes—they're too young. He's too young. Those eyes... I see the emptiness of loss in them. Those eyes look like mine. They aren't the eyes of the man that I know. The eyes I know are older. We're closer in age right now than we'll ever be—only ten or so years apart. It's an odd feeling, being so close to your dad like this. I wonder, briefly, if in a different time, we would've been friends. *If he wasn't my dad, and I wasn't his daughter, and we were the same age...* I shake my head and lean into the cushion of the sofa.

Dad nods numbly. "Will…will she remember who I am?"

"She…" I pause and set the empty bowl on top of the coffee table. "I'm not sure, honestly. I don't remember much from this time of my life…but eventually, yes. Eventually we come around."

I look past him toward the entryway, to the stairs. I cross my arms over my chest.

"It's a dark road ahead of you," I whisper. "You and I, we fight—a lot. Mostly because of me, I think… I can't promise you that it'll be pretty."

"But you're safe?"

The words, so soft and gentle, pull me from my thoughts, and I look up at him. He's got tears in his eyes. They drip past his eyelashes, down his cheek, then off his chin. He sucks in a shuddery breath.

"Just tell me—Lorrie will be safe."

I smile. My heart aches. "Yes, Dad…you keep her safe."

He collapses forward, his face in his palms, his shoulders defeated. He's alone now, I realize, and I have to press my palms tightly together to keep myself from crying.

"Oh, God, Lorraine," my dad heaves out a sob and scrubs the tears from his face. "What do I do? *What do we do?*"

I stand. I grab the box of junk and look at him. "Your best,

Dad. I can tell you that you've always done your best... I can't fault you for that."

I step away from him, holding the box of junk tight against my stomach, and close my eyes. I take one last deep breath of my childhood—smell the carpet cleaner my mom used to use, the one we stopped using ages ago. I clench my teeth. I feel electricity race up my arms and down my legs. It forms a ball at my center. I think of Buck. I think of my dad—not the man standing before me, but *my* dad. The brilliant, kind, wacky man. And in an instant, I'm gone from the past and back to where I belong.

Four Months Later

I SCROLL THROUGH MY PHONE as I absentmindedly stir the pot on the stove. I can hear my dad muttering in the living room of our small, two-bedroom apartment.

We made the move over two months ago, and the brown paper boxes are still stacked high around us. It'd been my idea to move. Closer to Columbus meant more job opportunities and a shorter commute to and from Columbus State Community College, where I'd enrolled. My dad had been more than ready to leave behind the basement, the TIME Machine, and all the stress the past nine years had held.

The TIME Machine is gone. Each piece was melted down, and the tachyon liquid was sealed and disposed of. My stomach churns whenever I think back to Huson Laboratory. The inventions and tests, and who knows what else, are still locked under dozens of underground floors.

But that's more of a "not my circus, not my monkeys" type deal. Uncle Sebastian, for his part, had immediately quit and gone to the police. He's neck-deep in a legal battle about secret government contracts and HIPAA violations. Dad and I had been worried about him at first, but Sebastian had quickly found his place among a group of protesters who were trying to raise public awareness of what exactly went on at Huson Labs. Each one has their own twisted story of some strange technology they'd been involved with—some strange invention that had, in one way or another, uprooted their lives. I'm pretty sure most of them are just conspiracy theorists, but then again…if it had happened to me…who else had it happened to?

Miller hasn't shown his face since that terrible night. I'd only seen him once, when the police had come and locked down our house again. He'd shown up in the crowd, a big white bandage on his neck, his sunglasses obscuring his face. He wore a new suit. He'd pulled me aside to "talk" and, in the end, Buck, Dad, and I all signed NDAs about the whole incident. I didn't mind. I was really done with this whole thing, anyway.

Sebastian had told me that, after I'd gone downstairs and destroyed the Machine, Miller had calmly gotten up, thanked him for removing the mind control device from his neck, and had promptly left.

I wonder, sometimes, about that small black square. The police had taken it as evidence. I don't understand how something so tiny can cause such a big problem, but then again, I never did understand the science behind those sorts of things.

I'm just an artist, after all.

Someone knocks on the door.

"Got it!" Dad calls. I glance at the doorway and grin as Buck walks in a second later.

"Hey, babe!" I turn back to the stove, stir the noodles a final time, then click the burner off. I turn back toward Buck right as he wraps his big, burly arms around me, and I lean into the embrace.

"I brought a movie for us to watch," he says.

I lean back and Buck holds up *Back to the Future*.

"Do you think you're funny?" I ask. Buck cackles, presses a kiss to the top of my head, and then walks into the living room. Seconds later, I hear my dad chuckle.

"Pasta's almost done!" I call. I grab the pot and pour the pasta into the colander in the sink, watching as the steam billows up from the noodles.

Time is a funny thing. It seems like it doesn't change for years until, suddenly, in a single instant, everything is different.

But maybe that's just the way life is supposed to be. Each

moment counts, even the mundane ones. They make up a person. I walk into the living room and lean against the doorway, watching Buck and Dad struggle to connect the TV to the DVD player.

I still miss Mom. I always will. I'll never be able to fully stop thinking about what life would be like if she were here through all of it. But even though my heart aches, and sometimes I find myself staying up late imagining the what-ifs...I have to admit, this life is still pretty good.

We grab our dinner and gather on the brown leather couch. We sit and watch the movie as we eat. I lean my head against Buck's shoulder, my feet curled up onto the sofa. My dad sits on my other side, his eyes trained on the screen as he spoons pasta into his mouth. Buck watches with a grin, his arm over me. I shut my eyes.

Lorrie will like this.

Acknowledgments

MY MENTOR ASKED ME if Lorraine believed in God... He certainly exists within the world of this story, and he certainly influenced the path she was on...but I don't think Lorraine even considered him a possibility in her life until *after* the events of the book. One night, as she fell asleep in her new apartment, she thought back on all the events, on this entire book you just read...and she saw where Jesus was with her. Dear reader, I don't know what you've gone through, who you've lost, or what your life looks like. But I do know this. God loves you. God wants a relationship with you. All you have to do is ask.

I didn't write this book. I mean, sure, my name is on the front cover. *Technically*, I wrote all the words. But the story as a whole wasn't all me. There are so many people who have helped this story come about, so many people who have influenced it.

I want to thank, first and foremost, my parents—specifically my Dad. You have encouraged me literally every single step of the way. You helped me figure out tachyons, you named the TIME Machine, and you let me read you the first five chapters when I was having a mental breakdown about the quality of writing—and assured me you loved it and couldn't wait to hold the book in your hands. I really couldn't have done any of this without you.

To my sister Katelyn, for once again providing me with a title. Seriously, *Call It Consequences* is a way better title than anything I could have come up with.

To Shelby, for listening to me rant about how this was *"the end of my writing career,"* and, *"Why did I ever think I could understand time travel?"* Thank you for telling me I could do this and for never hanging up the phone, despite the fact that I say the same thing about every story I've ever written.

To Lucy, for your insane amount of insight into the characters (and *me*), and for your extremely helpful developmental edit and copy edit. The book wouldn't be the same without your insight and dedication to your craft.

Brad Pauquette, you challenged me to write a Time Travel novel and wouldn't take, *"But I'm not smart enough,"* as an excuse to not even try. You never gave up on me, and you never let me give up on myself. Thank you.

To all those who helped produce the book, Levi Matthews, Noah Matthews, Lucy Grecu, and Vella Karman. You did a fantastic job!

This book wouldn't have been produced without my monthly supporters: Christina Silic, David Bartlett, David and Lydia Silic, Catherine Stringer, Heidi Thornhill, Kevin Prince, Katelyn Flatt, and Sam and Reece. Without your constant support, this book wouldn't have made it off my computer. Thank you!

My final thank you, of course, goes to God, the Holy Spirit, and Jesus Christ. Thank you for guiding me, thank you for loving me, thank you for saving me. I am so glad you understand time and that I am *not* in charge of this whole "life" thing—because my brain *hurt* after writing this. (If I'm being honest, it still kind of hurts.)

Until next time,

ALLI PRINCE

———————

P.S. Could you do me a favor? If you really liked this book (or even if you didn't), would you leave a review on Amazon or Goodreads? It would mean the world to me!

About the Author

ALLI PRINCE has been creating stories since she could form words and has been writing since long before she learned about sentence structure and grammar (her editors think she could still learn a thing or two about grammar).

She's the best-selling author of *Copper Lies* and *Lawless: An Anthology of Short Stories Inspired by the Book of Judges.*

When she isn't drafting or editing, you can see her encouraging others to commit arson against the enemy on her blog or watch her being a general menace to her friends on her Instagram. Go see what else she's up to at alliprince.com!

WANT TO WRITE LIKE ALLI?

Alli Prince is a graduate of The Company's full-time writing apprenticeship. She's now a bestselling author!

The apprenticeship is a college-alternative for motivated Christian writers. Our full-time, in-person program turns passionate young writers into published authors.

If you're ready to kick your writing into gear, learn more at: **Writers.Company**

WE HAVE SO MUCH MORE FOR YOU!

PEARLMAG.CO

Visit us and subscribe at PearlMag.co:

- New short stories, poetry, and essays regularly published online (all free!)

- More books to explore from genre-bending Christian authors

- Opportunities to submit your work and connect with other readers

www.ingramcontent.com/pod-product-compliance
Lightning Source LLC
Chambersburg PA
CBHW030644020726
47493CB00006B/1867